RETRIBUTION

AND OTHER TWISTED TALES

AMY KRISTOFF

Deer Run Press
Cushing, Maine

2010

Library of Congress Card Number: 2016935369

ISBN: 978-1-937869-05-2

First Printing, 2016, USA

Published by
Deer Run Press
8 Cushing Road
Cushing, ME 04563

Contents

Retribution

Martha Keims had no reason to suspect her youngest of three sons had an evil bone in his body. As a real estate agent, she'd been around many different kinds of people and considered herself all-knowing when it came to personalities. As it was, she ought to have known her boys.

Not to brag, but Martha was very successful and made a lot of money for her boss, Marty Ocher, the owner of "Colten Real Estate." She had often considered striking out on her own but "preferred to defer," not unlike in her marriage. Hopeless drunk though her husband was, he was the head of the household.

It was reassuring for Martha to think she passed on more positive than negative attributes to her kids, particularly Kory, the youngest. Her husband, Tim, didn't think having a third child was "necessary." (That was his line of thinking in his younger days, when he was sober.) At least then he was brusque but didn't have a temper. Over the years alcohol had evidently changed his brain chemistry. It had certainly changed his physical appearance. His carpentry work helped keep him in shape, but his beer gut was finally showing.

Tim's favorite place on earth was the sofa in the den, right in front of the TV. He acted like he owned them both, along with the remote. Martha had placed two expensive throw pillows on the sofa for decoration, and he had even laid claim to those, using one for his head and the other for his

1

feet. It was hard not to take that kind of behavior personal-ly.

Kory Keims felt like he'd been thrown to the wolves, the second his unaffectionate, alcoholic father declared Kory had one week of summer vacation following graduation from Pinecrest Junior and Senior High School. After that, it was expected he would "live on his own." In other words, Kory had to get the hell out of the house *and* support himself like it was second nature. His two older brothers, Chase and Brian, were more than ready to leave by the time they were eighteen. Both of them had part-time jobs since they were old enough to drive, while Kory had evidently been counting on some sort of reprieve.

If Kory had refused to leave home, his mother probably would have attempted to stand up for him, but she wouldn't have defended him for long. Kory's father was an expert at verbal abuse, which spared him from having to leave the sofa long enough to get physical. The sad part was Kory received the brunt of his father's verbal assaults over the years. Clenching his jaw was how Kory would in turn react, as he'd never talk back at his old man.

No amount of studying made Kory an "A-student" in even one subject. His brothers never studied and invariably got "B"s, even an "A" here and there. Sometimes it felt like once the teachers encountered Kory in their classes, they'd had enough of giving the Keim brothers "the benefit of the doubt." As if to reinforce their suspicions, Kory ended up being com-paratively dumb.

It was Kory's first day of work, and he hardly woke up in time. Already it was 7:25, and he was expected to "clock-in" at the "Frish's" supermarket in Colten, at eight A.M. There was more than one Frish's, but fortunately this particular one was where courtesy clerk help was most needed. It was the closest one to the basement apartment he was renting.

Otherwise he would have had to commute to either the one on the outskirts of Barrymoor or the one in Pinecrest, where he went to high school. Several small towns were included in the school district, so he rode the bus from Colten.

To help save time, Kory took a super-quick shower and put on his "uniform" (a short-sleeved, navy polo shirt and black jeans). Black pants were preferred over jeans, but he decided to wait until he was certain his job would be "permanent" before spending any money on an actual pair of black pants.

All Kory needed on a day like this, was to have his Ford Escort with 181,000 miles, refuse to start. Sure enough, it wouldn't. This wasn't unusual for it, but it was the first time he was left entirely to his own devices. If he called his mother, she'd be willing to drive across town and help him, but Kory's father would forbid her from doing so. Asking his landlady, Mrs. Camp, for help was out of the question, even if all he needed was a jump-start. She probably didn't have jumper cables, anyway.

Jogging to his first day of work at Frish's was Kory's only option. Provided he kept a steady pace, he expected to reach the supermarket no more than five minutes late.

After Kory had applied for the courtesy clerk position, he'd picked up a free paper advertising apartment rentals in the area. He found a one-bedroom, one-bath in the walk-out basement of the landlady's home. At $275.00 a month and no security deposit or yearly contract required, it was tempting to agree to rent it over the phone, especially since it was offered furnished, including dishes, towels and bed linens. Even the utilities were part of the rent.

The landlady, Mrs. Camp, had insisted Kory have a look at his future home before making a final decision. Besides, she wanted to meet him, although she said he sounded like a nice young man. She also liked the fact he would be employed at Frish's in Colten. Fortunately she didn't bother asking him what his position would be, although it was probably obvious.

Thanks to two years of high school cross-country train-
ing, Kory managed to clock-in at 7:58 A.M. Even though he
was out of breath, he hardly noticed because he was so
relieved not to be late.

Frish's had only been open an hour, and it appeared to
be pretty much empty. Possibly Kory was the only courtesy
clerk on duty for the time being. That notion initially made
him a little nervous, but he actually preferred that to having
another courtesy clerk hassle him. He'd been through
enough of that crap in school.

Unless directed otherwise, Kory was expected to bag groceries, so he headed for check stand five, where a long-haired
blonde cashier was scanning items like she knew what she
was doing. Although Kory had been in this store a few times
with his mother, he never saw this lady before.

The cashier turned when Kory approached, locking eyes
with him and exchanging smiles. She was beautiful and
wasn't even wearing any make-up. What really blew him
away was she was so calm. Meanwhile he was so stressed
he could hardly stand it.

None of the groceries had yet been bagged, so once Kory
got the O.K. from the customer to use plastic bags, he set to
work. In the meantime, after the cashier had pushed groceries in his direction a couple times, he finally got a glimpse
of her name tag: "Janette."

Since the first customer Kory bagged for didn't want
carry-out service, he went ahead and started bagging the
next order, which included two large frozen pizzas that
refused to fit in a plastic bag, not even singly. In nothing flat,
the groceries started piling up, flustering Kory.

Pausing long enough to push some more items in his
direction, Janette took the opportunity to ask him, "Is this
your first day?" Seeing Kory nod, she told him, "Even though

4

the customer wanted plastic bags, you can use the paper ones for the larger items."

Kory thanked her for the information and tried to catch up with the bagging duties. He was so intent on his task, he failed to notice another courtesy clerk approach and poke him on his left side, in his ribs.

"You new here?" Jeff asked, pulling his navy shirt out so Kory could read the name tag.

What Kory wanted to do was tell the twit, "Duh!" but didn't want to be a smart-ass on his first day, even if this idiot deserved it. Besides, with Janette close by, the last thing Kory wanted to do was make a bad impression.

After Kory had answered shortie Jeff's question, the latter refused to leave. Fortunately Janette stepped in, telling Jeff, "There's a whole cartload of take-backs by register one. And unless you're needed for courtesy service after that, you can mop the aisles."

The customer wanted carry-out service, and it had started raining like crazy. Kory had been too busy getting settled in his apartment to pay any attention to what the weather was supposed to do today. And since Mrs. Camp's house was surrounded by trees, it was hard to see much of the sky. It was sunny earlier, but it was possible there had been dark clouds on the horizon.

Ed Serla's office didn't have a window, but he was well-aware of the weather conditions and proceeded to stop Kory from going outside by grabbing his arm. It was the only way to stop the kid, given how intent he was on "doing his job." Ed didn't mind that at all; it was far better than having the kid f##k around, like some employees. A startled Kory was asked, "Would you like to borrow a hooded jacket so you don't get soaked? It might not be completely waterproof, but it's better than nothing."

After looking at the long, black vinyl raincoat of the customer for whom he was providing carry-out service, Kory took his boss up on the generous offer.

Amy Kristoff

As Kory made his way through the parking lot, following the fancy raincoat-wearing customer, he was already thinking about how soaking wet he would be if it decided to rain nonstop until his quitting time, four P.M. Then he had to walk home. Fortunately, however, he quickly completed the carry-out service and returned to the store before he got soaked. Mr. Serla's jacket definitely came in handy. Since the rain appeared to be letting up, Kory hopefully would no longer need it.

Mr. Serla wasn't in his office, so Kory placed the jacket on a black plastic chair with a silver metal frame, the only chair that didn't have a fabric back and seat. He'd been interviewed for his job in this same room, but he'd been too nervous to notice the many golf-related collectibles on his boss's desk and a black metal filing cabinet. The closest golf club was a public one with two eighteen-hole courses, located in Barrymoor. If Mr. Serla lived in Colten, he had to do some driving to reach it.

Emerging from the manager's office, Kory noticed someone had taken the cart he'd left outside, but he didn't think anything of it.

Myra Marshall at check stand eight, did not like Jeff Savage, the worst courtesy clerk ever to work at the Colten Frish's. She'd been a full-time cashier at this store for close to twelve years, so she felt like she was in the know. Savage only had a job here because his uncle was Rod Frish, the owner. Savage's parents owned the "Beaufort's" restaurant here in town, and she couldn't imagine why he didn't work there. However, it was rumored he worked there, too. Still, Myra couldn't imagine that miscreant working hard. She'd never gone to his family's restaurant because it was too expensive.

There was a new courtesy clerk helping Myra, and since she had yet to see Jeff Savage, she hoped he got the boot, although that sounded too good to be true. Meanwhile, she asked the new bagger, "You're new here, aren't you? This your first day?"

Kory told her he was "new" and indeed, it was his first day. He'd already figured out it was imperative to be polite to the cashiers; they were the key to maintaining equilibrium around here. The manager, Mr. Serla, was seemingly hardly ever around.

Since the customer wanted carry-out service, Kory was compelled to turn and look out the windows to see if it was raining again. The elderly lady-customer told him, "Don't worry about getting wet, young man. I don't believe it's raining, and I happen to have a temporary handicap parking tag on my rearview mirror, so my car's basically as close to the entrance as you could hope."

Returning to the store, Kory was two bucks richer, thanks to that kindly old woman. He wouldn't have minded getting soaking wet from a downpour, just for that tip. He couldn't help noticing the jacket Mr. Serla had lent him, remained where Kory had left it.

The cashier who Kory had just helped was no longer at her register, so Janette at number five was back to having the only check stand open. Since he was still on bagging duty, he went over to help her. As it was, Jeff was nowhere to be seen. Possibly he was still doing take-backs.

Janette's current customer had a very large order, and Janette had already bagged several of the items, which Kory placed in the customer's cart before getting to work. As soon as the customer finally noticed plastic bags were being used, she remarked, "I'd prefer you bag the remainder of my order using paper, please."

Not surprisingly, the snobby lady-customer wanted carry-out service, so Kory dutifully followed her out to her vehicle. He'd expected her to be driving something really ritzy but instead had an older, faded-maroon Ford Taurus. Still, she had so much attitude! It was amazing not even the junker she drove brought her down a couple notches.

Relieved to be finished with that particular customer, Kory hurried back to the store, only to have Jeff Savage meet him in the entryway and tell him Mr. Serla wanted to have a word with him.

"Why?" Kory asked, thinking aloud.

Jeff pointed upward and declared, "All I know is he just called you to his office, over the P.A."

That bit of information made Kory momentarily feel faint. The last thing he ever wanted to do was draw attention to himself. Next to that, he absolutely did not want to make Mr. Serla mad.

Kory's boss was seated behind his desk. As usual the office door had been wide open, so Kory didn't hesitate to walk right in. The second he sat down, Mr. Serla got up and shut the door. Kory felt very ill.

Kory had one day's pay in his pocket, although it was a check, not cash. He was allowed to work until four P.M., as he was originally scheduled to do, even though he was technically fired at about ten-twenty A.M., accused of having stolen "a golf ball clock" from his boss's office. The ridiculous part was Kory couldn't imagine what the hell a golf ball clock looked like. When he'd stated as much (minus the word "hell"), Mr. Serla impatiently retorted, "It's an actual golf ball with a clock face, attached to an oak base. It happened to be a Father's Day gift from one of my daughters, a few years back."

O.K.! Kory got it. He didn't need to hear any elaboration describing something that he never saw in the first place and would certainly never steal. Nevertheless, this marked the end of his first job. It figured he couldn't last even one day. Obviously his mother was right to feel protective of him. Thanks to her, there was a couple hundred dollars in his bank account, and his first month's rent had been paid.

That was her graduation present to him, although she claimed it was also a gift from her alcoholic husband. Kory knew that was a lie.

What Kory intended to do was walk to "Colten Bank" and deposit his check. Fortunately the sky was partly-cloudy, and it didn't look like it would be raining again anytime soon. The bank was in fact even further from his apartment than the supermarket, but he decided to look around and see if anyone was hiring. It was unthinkable to fail at self-sufficiency; his father would positively relish having his youngest son come crawling back home.

Only after Kory left the bank with nothing but a deposit receipt did he realize he'd made no provision for dinner. There was nothing in the refrigerator at the apartment, and he had little more on him than the two dollars' tip he'd received earlier in the day. Truthfully he was so upset he wasn't hungry anyway, despite having not eaten yet today. Maybe he'd get lucky and find another job before heading home. He still had his broken down car to deal with, but it was one thing at a time at this point. There was no chance he'd ask his parents for any help on that matter, not even his mother.

At the northeast corner of Main and East Streets, there was an upscale restaurant, "Beaufort's," where Kory considered applying for a busboy position. Assuming he'd have to walk to and from work indefinitely, this place was no more than half a mile further from his apartment than Frish's. His mother had taken some of her clients there for lunch and had raved about the food, although the service was sometimes wanting. Maybe he could help change that.

The restaurant was located in a large, square, flat-roofed, white plaster building that was formerly an automotive repair shop. Given all the quaint touches, such as pink geraniums in white wooden window boxes and black shutters on either side of the paned windows that faced Main Street, it was hard to guess the building's original use. Although the entrance was in the front, the asphalt parking area was in the back.

There were no hours of business posted anywhere, so Kory went ahead and tried the door, which was made of heavy planks of wood, painted white. It stuck at first, but he pushed on it until it opened.

What Kory initially noticed upon entering the gray, slate-tiled dining room, was the heavy metal music booming throughout. Also, there wasn't a soul in the place. Before seeing who posed the question, Kory was asked, "Can I help you?" and was told the restaurant wasn't open again until five-thirty. Then, who appeared but Jeff from Frish's. Kory was stunned to see that idiot, never mind how the jerk pretended not to recognize him.

Kory decided to play right along and managed to keep a straight face and his voice level while saying, "No, I don't think you can help me." He couldn't leave that place fast enough, although he tried to look like he didn't have a care in the world.

Once outside, Kory wasn't in such a hurry and in fact was suddenly curious about something. He headed to the parking lot, where there was a single vehicle – a two-door, tan Chevy Cavalier. It had to be Jeff's. Since both windows were wide open, it was worth it to have a look. Sure enough, on the dirty-looking, tan cloth seat, there was a fancy-looking golf ball clock. Finally Kory knew what "the stolen goods" looked like.

Unless there was a video camera recording what Kory just did, he was home free, as there wasn't a single window behind the restaurant. After placing the clock under his shirt, he headed back to his apartment. This was more rewarding than landing a new job, for the time being, at least.

With plenty of time to think, Kory wondered why he'd never seen Jeff in school, assuming he was close to the same age. Maybe he was several years older and only looked rather young. Possibly he lived in another school district or attended a parochial school. He might have even been home-schooled. That never could have happened for any of the Keims' sons because their mother was too busy and their father didn't give half a damn.

The more Kory thought about everything, why would Mr. Serla have any reason to believe Kory retrieved the stolen golf ball clock from the passenger seat of "the thief's" car? There didn't seem to be any way of winning this one.

Janette was rinsing the dinner dishes, readying them for the dishwasher, when she suddenly felt like someone was watching her. Since it was almost dark and she never closed the shade for the kitchen window above the sink, it was entirely possible an individual could see her much more eas-ily than she could see him. Fortunately it wasn't as if she ever dressed provocatively when standing here, doing what-ever task. As it was, only her upper half could have been vis-ible from outside. However, sometimes her husband, Scott, came up behind her in the evening and put his arms around her and started kissing the back of her neck.

The thing was, Scott only did that if he was in a good mood, and his mood at times appeared to be based on the alignment of the stars. It was the only conclusion Janette could draw about her husband's unpredictability, after almost fifteen years of marriage. It wasn't like she was into astrology; the bottom line was her husband had a problem controlling his temper/emotions, which put a strain on their marriage. But she didn't believe in divorce. As awful as it sounded, someone would have to kill her husband before she'd give up on him.

After rinsing the last dinner plate, Janette leaned over to place it in the dishwasher and simultaneously felt a hand on her lower back. She wasn't expecting this, given the horrible mood Scott had been in when he returned home from his job

11

at the Colten post office. He was planning on being promoted, only to find out he'd been passed over. Janette never in a million years would have told him this, but she was amazed he'd managed to keep the same job for almost as long as they'd been married. He'd confessed to "learning how to relax" thanks to her, and when they first met he claimed to already be on his twentieth job.

As Janette stood up straight, she couldn't help looking out the window, trying to confirm if anyone was out there. Meanwhile, Scott started kissing the back of her neck, pushing her ponytail out of the way. Soon she was so aroused it was difficult to complete her after-dinner tasks. Somehow she wiped the sink and the counter area around it, even though she was being driven insane with Scott's kisses and caresses. Still attempting to see who the peeping tom was, Janette finally "spied" the culprit: none other than the courtesy clerk Kory, from Frish's! It turned out he didn't appear to be spying but was pacing back and forth at the end of the driveway, debating about approaching the house and ringing the doorbell. She felt badly about him being fired his first day on the job, but he deserved it for stealing a piece of golf memorabilia from the boss's office. As it was, she'd been wondering why Kory had suddenly avoided her, after initially gravitating to her check stand.

Whatever Kory's reason for coming around here, the problem was Scott. If the latter had any idea there was "a young man from work" loitering outside the house, he'd chase him down and pummel him. Usually Janette's only concern about these make-out sessions was whether one of their two kids might walk in on them. They were ensconced in front of the TV in the den, downstairs, typically staying put until bath and bedtime in another hour and a half.

Just as Janette was about to turn around, hoping to keep Scott from looking outside, he did just that. "Who the hell's out there?" he practically yelled, immediately halting the romancing. Nothing good with him lasted long. Thankfully

she was accustomed to that part of being married to him, but she couldn't begin to predict how this current dilemma would conclude, once "the chasing and pummeling" was out of the way.

All Kory had wanted (what little it amounted to in his mind) was to leave Mr. Serla's golf ball clock with Janette from Frish's. Kory had decided on this plan after much thought, and he spoke about it with his landlady, Mrs. Camp. She was amazing, how patiently she listened to his story about having been framed by Jeff Savage and afterward being accused of something he didn't do, resulting in him being fired. She believed he was indeed innocent and sided with him about the necessity of making sure the stolen golf ball clock was returned to Mr. Serla. She knew him, and she also knew Janette, whose last name was "Long." Coincidentally Janette and her family lived near the very end of Justine Way, the same street where Mrs. Camp's house was.

It was dusk when Kory followed the sidewalk to Janette's, having been told by Mrs. Camp the house was a mustard-colored tri-level on the same side of the street as her own house. Justine Way was a dead-end, and the Long residence was the third from the last residence. Kory had been grateful for so much help from Mrs. Camp and found inspiration from it.

At first it seemed like a great idea to give Janette the golf ball clock, once Kory explained himself. Mrs. Camp told him Janette was "super understanding" and would believe his story. Kory was emboldened by the assurance and when he reached Janette's house, it was unnerving to see her in the kitchen window, apparently washing dishes or cleaning up. As darkness seemed to fall more and more rapidly, he became increasingly anxious and ended up pacing back and forth in front of the house.

The next thing Kory knew, a light over the front stoop came on, and the front door flew open. Before anyone even appeared, a man yelled, "Get over here, you shit!"

Kory took off running in the direction of his apartment, nearly losing the golf ball clock on more than one occasion. At some point, he in fact considered whipping the damned thing into the shrubs of this or that house. But he didn't want to "lose his head" and do something impulsive. He needed the evidence to vindicate himself; otherwise he'd never get another job in this town.

It was time for another plan, was all. This was when he wished he were clever and smart, versus just plain dumb. Being the latter came in handy when he was still considered "a kid." Now that he'd been hurled into adulthood, he was suddenly expected to be "an adult." The thought made him sick. Nonetheless, he was actually glad he was fired from his job at Frish's. (He was determined to see a bright side to what unfairly happened to him.) This way, he knew what being fired felt like, so he had that under his belt.

Finally out of breath, Kory walked the rest of the way to his apartment, the golf ball clock still under his shirt. Mrs. Camp's house was only a few dozen yards ahead, and fortunately no one was pursuing him. He almost didn't care, given how close he was to "home."

There happened to be a street light in front of Mrs. Camp's house, which helped illuminate her property, along with a few outside fixtures. Kory would have seen his mother's maroon Buick La Crosse, parked behind his Escort, even if it'd been pitch black. He walked right up to her car, expecting to find her sitting behind the wheel, blabbing in the dark on her cell phone. Instead, she was nowhere to be seen. Mrs. Camp must have invited her inside, so the two could chat while waiting for Kory to return. He just hoped Mrs. Camp didn't tell his mother why he was out for awhile. He expected she'd keep that confidential. Given how shameless Kory's mother was about offering her real estate services, she was probably doing "a free market analysis" of Mrs. Camp's house.

That would take some time, Kory concluded, heading for the door of his apartment, located to the right of where the two cars were parked. Once he let himself in, he'd only close the storm door, so his mother would know he was home. He'd also turn on the light by the door, which operated on a switch that was separate from the other outside light fixtures.

Just as Kory was about to unlock the door, it was opened by none other than his mother, who enthusiastically greeted him and made as if to hug him. Apparently she'd been waiting in his apartment for his return. Mrs. Camp must have let her in, as he'd made sure to lock the door. It took everything Kory had, to acknowledge her with a mere grunt, which was completely unlike him. He'd never disrespected either parent, even though he'd been compelled to do so on many occasions, in regard to his drunk father.

The bottom line: all the effort Kory had been going to, to prove he was an adult, and this was his reward? He didn't blame Mrs. Camp for letting his mother into the apartment; he blamed his mother for putting him in this predicament. She needed to stand up to her husband, inform him their youngest son wasn't ready to immediately become self-sufficient. Since she just invaded his privacy, maybe she ought to be the one who returned the golf ball clock.

Kory pulled the clock out from under his shirt, only now realizing it was heavy enough to be a weapon. As his mother turned and went into *his apartment, ahead* of him, it became obvious she deserved to pay for everything that had happened. Even though he was her youngest and dumbest son, it didn't mean he couldn't make his point, right over the back of her head, using plenty of emphasis.

Amy Kristoff

Fore!

On his way to members-only Arrowhead Country Club in St. Charles, Illinois, a western suburb of Chicago, Jay Creel intended to inquire about tennis lessons for his wife, Daniela. He'd wanted to take this drive a couple weeks ago but didn't want to rush to judgment regarding his wife's choice of a riding instructor. However, given what Jay witnessed from the window of his home office, which overlooked the barn and riding arena, it was safe to conclude it was time to put a stop to her dream of becoming a competitive dressage rider. Supposedly there were several "levels" of proficiency, but she could just start thinking of another hobby. Her German trainer appeared to believe he had to make passes at her at every available opportunity. Didn't the moron realize who paid for the damned private lessons, as well as who built the two-stall barn, paddock, and riding ring? It was all to please his third wife, who seemed sincere, unlike cheating wives one and two. At least they attempted to keep their dalliances secret.

Although Jay had never yearned for kids, having someone to grow old with was of the utmost importance to him. And he was happy to share his wealth, although he'd learned from experience to have Daniela sign a pre-nuptial agreement. She was 27 to his 45, so it was highly probable she'd outlive him. Then she could have all the riding lessons she wanted, letting a hot male riding instructor put the moves on her. It wasn't like she needed anyone to teach her how to take care of her two horses, which she seemed to acquire in

16

no time at all. Bonnie Hall, a horsy friend of hers, helped her locate the two big, rangy mounts that supposedly originally came all the way from Europe. They were "only" twenty-grand apiece, and Jay was assured they were "bargains." He'd been "too in love" to think that was a lot of money. And that was after he'd built the barn and everything else these two herbivores required. Love wasn't blind; it potentially made you go broke, was all.

As far as the notion of tennis lessons for Daniela: she played competitively while attending Pinto High School in Scottsdale, Arizona. Her mother, Lynn, had been quite a successful professional player herself and encouraged her daughter to follow in her footsteps. Daniela had actually been more interested in taking riding lessons but had to set-tle for helping out on the weekends at a trail riding stable.

Anyway, the bottom line was Jay was doing something unprecedented as a husband, by taking the initiative to tell his third wife what her "lesson money" should be spent on. If she wanted someone to help her with her horses, she could have Bonnie do so – for free, since she technically wasn't a riding instructor. She sure as hell could be a know-it-all, not just about horses. Sometimes Jay wished his wife wasn't even friends with that woman. Bonnie was on her third mar-riage, just like Jay. But in that woman's case, she was just sucking her husbands dry financially and moving on, while Jay was the one being preyed upon. The verdict was still out on Daniela, but it wasn't looking good.

Unfortunately, Daniela had no interest whatsoever in golf and rolled her eyes whenever Jay had invited her to ride along in the golf cart for nine holes. He never even got to the point of inviting her to try hitting a few balls at the driving range. It would have positively floored him to have the opportunity to give Daniela some golf lessons. He wasn't anywhere close to an expert, but he'd started playing when he was seven. His father, Steven, would take him along to play nine holes at "Spring Valley," a public course in Geneva, where Jay grew up, not far from St. Charles.

Finally Jay reached the entrance to Arrowhead Country Club, a towering, white brick pillar on each side. Each one was topped by a round, concrete planter, filled with an assortment of colorful flowers. As soon as his blue Cadillac Escalade passed through the entryway, the parking lot initially appeared empty. Once in the confines of the country club, it suddenly appeared as if there was a golf tournament and a wedding reception taking place. It was weird, having a hundred or more vehicles materialize seemingly out of nowhere.

The course was "closed" on Mondays, to allow any members to reserve the course for a corporate outing or for the club to schedule a tournament of its own for the benefit of a certain group of members, such as "The Father's Day-After," which was a nine-hole tournament, followed by an outdoor luncheon with an awards ceremony. However, that wasn't until next week. If a member showed up on Monday, wanting to play golf, he or she had to either carry his or her golf bag or pay the fee to use a pull-cart. A caddie was possibly available, should the pro or his assistant (whoever was working on an "off" day) be able to contact one who was available on short notice. In the middle of summer, it was actually pretty easy to find one ready to work, even on a day off.

Jay ended up parking his Escalade at the far end of the parking lot, the only place where several spaces remained. Nonetheless, he was actually quite close to his destination, the tennis pro shop. Whenever he came to Arrowhead, he either played golf or had dinner with Daniela in the English hunting lodge-style clubhouse, so parking here on the east side was a new thing.

There also happened to be a snack bar in the same, rustic wood-sided building as the tennis pro shop. The front of the snack shop had a walk-up counter and a patio area, with three brown metal picnic tables, to accommodate the golfers taking a break between "the front and back nine." For the tennis players, there was a larger patio area behind the snack bar, with six round, black metal tables, each of which seated four. There was no need for umbrellas over any of the tables for either the front or back patios, as several large oak trees provided plenty of shade.

The back patio was soon reached after Jay had passed the four tennis courts. He wondered why no one was playing on such a beautiful day. It was sunny, the temperature was about 70 degrees, and there was little humidity. This was the first time Jay had ever approached "the halfway house" from this direction. Usually he played the front nine and walked along the paved path between the ninth green and the tenth tee, the latter of which was easily viewed from the front patio of the snack bar. And he only ever walked on the path, never rode in a cart. Even though he liked having a caddie, he made do with a pull-cart on Mondays.

A long and straight par-four, best described the tenth hole. It wasn't challenging unless you couldn't hit a drive at least 150 yards, particularly regarding the women's tee. If you teed off from the men's, you really had to nail it or be guaranteed of ending up at least one over par – and that was provided you got within chipping distance of the green with the second shot. The dilemma consisted of a canal that cut across the fairway, about fifty yards shy of the green.

Jay stood a few feet in front of the snack bar counter, unable to help but stare longingly at the tenth hole, not a single golfer in sight. What the hell happened? If all those vehicles were in the parking lot, there had to be something going on, especially since the snack bar was apparently open.

Whatever the case, it was time to confess because Jay couldn't take it anymore: ever since he accidentally killed a caddie by hitting a first tee shot out of bounds (and hitting the kid in the head), he had exiled himself from playing even nine holes here at Arrowhead. As much as he liked golf, he still couldn't get excited about playing any other courses. He loved the course here. He felt completely at home whenever he played it. And since he hadn't even swung a club for two months, it was suddenly very tempting to run back to the storage room behind the golf pro shop and grab his clubs. Since there was no one even close to approaching the tenth tee, he could hurry back here and play that hole and a couple more. He hadn't carried his own bag since he was young, but he was up to the challenge.

Because no charges were filed against him for "the incident," Jay felt more horrible than ever. The worst part was he had been feeling more guilty by the day, which was extremely unnerving. To top it off, he had the unwarranted situation involving his wife laying the groundwork for an affair. Maybe he was jumping to conclusions, but it was difficult not to do so after having his first two wives cheat on him.

Jay wasn't sure if the tennis pro shop was open, but the golf pro shop was, seven days a week, year-round. He in fact liked nothing more than to stop in the pro shop on a cold January or February afternoon, to check out the latest putters and other accessories.

Reaching the glass door of the tennis pro shop, it was unlocked. There didn't appear to be a sign posted, indicating the hours the store was open, unlike the golf pro shop.

Inside the shop, the first thing Jay noticed was how crammed it was with merchandise. There was an entire wall devoted to racks filled with a seemingly endless variety of women's attire, while there were two circular racks just of clearance-priced clothing. Having worked in retail before starting his consulting career, he appreciated the whole layout of the store, as well as that of the golf pro shop.

Looking over the women's clothing more closely, Jay couldn't help thinking about how Daniela would look in the "sexier" outfits. That sounded shallow, but his wife had a great figure and was very pretty. Her looks had been what initially attracted him, but he fell in love with her (apparent) sincerity. Maybe he was just being paranoid about her and that trainer. Ever since accidentally hitting that caddie with an out-of-bounds tee shot, Jay had felt like shit about everything. It was as if he "got off the hook" for unintentionally killing a person, yet some sort of punishment was awaiting him. Perhaps it was "all in his head," but that was the most disturbing possibility. Jay preferred to die than be declared insane and in turn forced to spend the remainder of his life in a mental institution. As long as he felt like this, he could never again play golf here at Arrowhead Country Club. And that meant he might as well not even exist.

"Can I help you, sir?" a tall, attractive brunette asked Jay, having approached him seemingly out of nowhere.

Jay replied, "I stopped in to inquire about private tennis lessons for my wife. She was quite a competitor in her youth, so I'd like to get her to renew her passion, versus having her take dressage lessons on her horses. Now that the barn's built, I don't mind her owning them, but that's as far as it needs to go."

The woman's face lit up and she said, "My sister rode dressage at a college in Virginia, way back when. I remember our mother forbidding her from trying any jumping-related disciplines, but Jenny still managed to fall off and break her collarbone at some point, proving falling off a horse is sometimes unavoidable."

Jay had to laugh at that comment, and he felt better about this "mission" of his. When he got home, he could tell Daniela how worried he was about her safety, and he wanted her to keep her horses "for fun" and quit worrying about trying to prove something.

The phone rang, so Ms. Brunette excused herself to answer it. The phone was apparently located somewhere behind the L-shaped glass counters in the far right corner of the store. Jay ended up essentially following her, to have a look at what was offered there: men's and women's watches, as well as an assortment of earrings, bracelets, and pendants

—most of which had a tennis theme. There were also bejeweled, tennis-themed coin purses, fanny packs and wrist wallets.

Looking over everything, Jay considered purchasing something for Daniela, just to let her know he'd thought of her. Then he remembered she was the whole reason he was here in the first place! He was in fact supposed to be furious with her for purportedly allowing an affair to start, practically right in front of him.

The dilemma was Jay loved his wife. He would simply have to give her the benefit of the doubt when dealing with her new trainer. Here on out, Jay would make sure to pay more attention to her, versus giving her space, which she supposedly craved.

Ms. Brunette's call finished, she pulled out a spiral date book and asked, "Would your wife like to come tomorrow morning at nine? Larry, my husband, also has an opening at one-thirty."

"How convenient," Jay remarked. The tennis instructor's wife could take the remark whatever way she wanted, but it was a relief to know there was someone to look out for possible "antics" on the court during lessons.

On second thought, what the hell was he thinking? Jay ended up saying he'd have to "go home and talk to his wife" before making an appointment. He hated to lack resolve, but it certainly wouldn't help his marriage if he forced Daniela to take up tennis again, since she obviously didn't miss it. Besides, in this case it sounded like (potentially) "more of the same."

The tennis pro's wife handed Jay a business card and told him to call to schedule a lesson for his wife, whenever she was ready. Or she was welcome to call or stop in, herself. They were looking forward to it.

Taking the business card and putting it in the left front pocket of his khakis, Jay thanked her and left, not bothering to look at what she handed him, as he was busy thinking about the woman's last statement. Maybe it was her strange tone of voice when she said it.

Lingering on the patio in front of the tennis pro shop and the snack shop, Jay didn't see a single player approaching the tenth tee, nor did he see any players on or nearing the ninth green. Then he turned around to confirm whether or not the business hours were posted on the front entrance of the tennis shop. He didn't even notice because his eyes zeroed in on the counter of the snack bar, where the tan metal shutter was closed. He could have sworn it was open when he looked before.

Obviously there was no golf tournament, so any players on the course, consisted of members willing to play with "the bare necessities": no caddies, unless a special request was made; no riding carts; and no snack bar. For the sake of his peace of mind, Jay had to go to the clubhouse and see what was going on, to result in so many vehicles being parked in the large parking lot. After that he was going home, where he expected his wife had avoided "getting into trouble" with her new dressage trainer.

Naturally Jay used the paved cart path to reach his destination, as it ran straight from the tennis pro shop and snack bar to the rear entrance of the clubhouse's "Main Dining Room." He could hardly keep from breaking into a jog, but he didn't want to look like he was hurrying. Then again, who would see him?

As Jay was nearing the back of the first tee, he slowed his rapid walking pace and got a good look at not only the first fairway but the eighteenth green, to the left of the first tee. At the moment there wasn't a player in sight.

After a couple minutes, a twosome approached the ninth green, to the distant right of the first tee. The center of that green was where the caddie was standing when Jay had accidentally hit him. That had definitely been one hell of an out-of-bounds tee shot. The irony was he'd never before hit a ball out-of bounds on the first tee. He rarely did so on any tee, not that he was a great golfer.

Jay had unintentionally stopped walking by this time, so intent was he on observing the two players finish the front nine. The closer they got, it appeared there was a single player and a caddie.

That wasn't right, Jay decided, as he continued to watch the twosome. The purported caddie just swung a club while simultaneously balancing a full-sized golf bag on his right shoulder. Jay couldn't wait to see where the ball landed.

Daniela drove to Arrowhead Country Club as if she were an ambulance driver on the way to the scene of an accident. Normally she wasn't an aggressive driver by any means, but the current situation required it. She needed to find her husband, Jay, and reassure him if he saw anything questionable from his office window at home, involving some flirting between her and a riding instructor who made house calls, he had it all wrong. The guy turned out to be a low-life creep, and she sent him packing shortly after Jay abruptly left. All she could think about was how Jay went to great expense to build a barn, turn-out area, and a riding ring for her two horses. She was well-aware he'd preferred not having to remove several large oak trees to make those additions to the two-acre property. It wasn't Daniela's fault her husband's first two wives cheated on him, which made him jump to ridiculous conclusions. As it was, if Daniela's mother had let her daughter take riding lessons instead of tennis lessons, maybe Daniela would have gotten the riding bug out of the way, sooner. Instead, she was allowed to help out at a stable and that was about it. Meanwhile, tennis lessons were jammed down her throat.

It was compelling to drive even faster once Daniela was almost to the country club. As she passed through the brick pillars of its entrance, she felt a new wave of urgency. Most of the very large parking lot was visible from this point – and it was nearly empty – yet she couldn't see Jay's blue Cadillac Escalade, which was nearly identical to her white one. It should have been parked near the golf pro shop. After all, on any given Monday during "golf season," where would he be but playing nine or even eighteen holes here at Arrowhead?

On second thought, ever since what happened a couple months ago . . . It wasn't Jay's fault his first tee shot hit a caddie in the head, killing the kid. And the caddie was on another hole, so obviously it wasn't like Jay did it on purpose. Fortunately the investigators saw it that way too, and the caddie's family didn't file a lawsuit against anyone. Nevertheless, Jay had felt absolutely tortured ever since that day, although he'd been pretending to feel fine. He did, however, confess to not wanting to play golf "for awhile," which meant he wouldn't be playing here at his beloved Arrowhead. It was like a second home for him, so she'd taken her chances that was still the case. Considering his simple desires made Daniela love him more than ever.

Finally Jay's SUV was spotted, parked even with the tennis pro shop and the courts, except the vehicle was on the opposite side of the parking lot. That was strange because the only time Jay liked to walk was while playing a round of golf. One reason he'd never splurged on a fancy sports car was he'd always be compelled to park at the far end of every parking lot.

Daniela parked her Escalade next to her husband's, hoping to see him suddenly appear. She even looked in the windows and tried the doors. Of course they were locked, and she didn't see him anyway. Standing here, she was about even with the sidewalk that passed the four tennis courts and led to the pro shop, as well as a snack shop that catered to both the tennis players and the golfers. She walked toward the end of the sidewalk, where it met a paved cart path that ran both right and left. Once there, she turned right and started walking toward the golf pro shop, hoping Jay was inside, looking at clubs. Purchasing a new set would hopefully inspire him to play again. Not playing was seriously depressing him.

Looking in the direction of the course, Daniela attempted to focus on the few players, but they were too far away. Obviously this particular Monday was indeed a slow one, as there wasn't even a scheduled tournament of some kind.

Because Daniela was not only staring out at the course but was preoccupied, she proceeded to practically fall over Jay's body, lying face-up about halfway between the first and tenth tees. Her first response was to cry out in shock, but she was soon kneeling beside him, checking his pulse. He was dead! It didn't seem possible, as he was still relatively young and in good shape. The only solace was his smile; he looked completely at peace.

Finally noticing the bump on Jay's forehead, Daniela looked around, wondering who could have accidentally hit him with a ball but wasn't even aware? Then again, did it really matter? Her husband was gone, and of course whoever hit him didn't do so on purpose. As it was, Jay might have gotten hit and was approached by the golfer who'd hit the errant ball. He probably told the player he was fine, and that was that. Suddenly, however, he fainted, lost consciousness, and . . .

Daniela started crying as she continued kneeling over Jay. She just wished she could have told him she loved him before he'd abruptly left the house earlier, in a completely needless huff.

After a few minutes, Daniela had enough crying. As she was about to stand, out of the corner of her eye she noticed a small, rectangular piece of white paper, in the shape of a business card, about to fall out of the left front pocket of Jay's khakis. She looked it over, finding it blank on both sides. Without thinking, she placed the paper in the left pocket of her breeches.

Crazy Quilt Society

Left at the altar on her wedding day, Mandy Snodgrass was forced to wonder what she'd done to deserve such punishment. All she'd wanted from a husband was reciprocal love and respect. Evidently she'd counted on the wrong individual.

Recently Mandy celebrated her 30th birthday with her mother, Gayle, who took her to lunch in Toledo. It was the farthest Mandy had been from her home in Plainfield (also in Ohio), in quite a long time. However, Toledo wasn't more than twenty miles away. Mandy was too dedicated to working full-time and sometimes time and a half at Golden Crescent Bakery (on Main) to have an opportunity to venture far.

Interestingly, almost everyone Mandy had invited to the wedding showed up, while only a few her fiancé invited, did—but not his mother. Obviously they'd been tipped off. Meanwhile, Mandy could have saved the trouble and expense of renting the banquet hall at the church she'd formerly attended. It was impossible to go back there, ever since what happened (or didn't). Nonetheless, it wasn't as if Mandy could completely avoid everyone, considering she was employed at a very popular bakery. Customers had been coming from farther away than Mandy was aware, until some had pointed out as much. Knowing that made her even more proud to work at Golden Crescent Bakery.

If Mandy ever attended church services again, she would have to find a place of worship a long way from the suffocat-

27

ing confines of "quaint" Plainfield. For the time being, she was getting in her socializing as a volunteer for "The Women Who Quilt Like Crazy Society." The name of the "society" had put Mandy off at first. After thinking about her life, she realized joining this quilting club was what she needed to help her get out of her mental rut.

Ever since starting her job at the bakery, Mandy had wanted to work as many hours as possible, not only for the money but to stay busy. Joining "The Women Who Quilt Like Crazy Society" not only helped keep her occupied but put her life in perspective. Because the society's quilts were made "upon request," there were intervals when the group didn't meet at all. Once they did, however, it was often necessary to work seemingly nonstop until the requested quilt was completed.

Because Mandy usually worked a midnight shift, typically she would go to bed once she returned home from work, around seven in the morning (unless she worked overtime). It was difficult for her to sleep for any duration, so she'd taken to sleeping a couple hours here and there, throughout the day. Coincidental or not, she'd had this problem ever since experiencing a case of amnesia, following an "incident" involving her former fiancé, Tad.

One of Tad's biggest faults (besides his general flakiness), was his lack of driving skills. Worse, he considered himself an exemplary driver and was incapable of believing otherwise, despite having numerous fender-benders and assorted citations. The only time he appeared focused was when his mother was talking to him. Somehow she never failed to garner his full attention.

Shortly after Mandy had accepted Tad's marriage proposal (but there wasn't a ring at the time because he'd wanted to take her shopping for it), he took her on a weekend skiing trip to northern Michigan. He was in graduate school at the time and didn't have many opportunities for a getaway. Meanwhile, Mandy was a receptionist at a dentist's office in

Jasper, which was about ten miles from Plainfield. Tad happened to be from Jasper and was a patient of the dentist, Dr. Perkins, who was the matchmaker for the two, thanks to Tad's inquiry about Mandy. At the time, she'd been extremely grateful for her employer's willingness to give Tad her phone number.

On their ill-fated ski trip, Mandy and Tad were staying at a vacation home owned by a close friend of Tad's. Even though the guy didn't have many opportunities to visit it in the winter, he made sure it was kept clean and was maintained. Also, the four-wheel drive pick-up truck was in running condition. That was helpful because the truck would be necessary for Mandy and Tad to reach the ski resort, as it had snowed a few inches overnight. Previously Mandy had found it "funny" Tad was allowed to use his friend's truck, given the fact he was such a reckless driver.

Once Tad had backed the truck out of the carport, Mandy finally emerged from the house. Barely had she gotten in, and he spun the truck around, narrowly avoiding sideswiping his beloved, snow-covered Camaro. What did he do but laugh and declare, "I'm starved! We gotta get some breakfast before anything else."

Mandy nodded while trying to find the seatbelt, which seemed to have disappeared. As Tad finished backing around the main part of the driveway, she glanced in his direction and noticed his seatbelt was secured, yet he detested wearing one and preferred "taking his chances," in regard to being injured or killed in an accident or being pulled over by a cop for failing to wear one.

Before Mandy had a chance to ask Tad if he knew about a possible missing seatbelt on the passenger side of what was probably a twenty-year-old truck, he somehow made it feel like it was literally flying down the winding, pine tree-lined drive. After managing to catch her breath, she asked him, "Are you in four-wheel drive?"

"I'm in neutral!" Tad replied, sounding jubilant.

Amy Kristoff

For a hundred yards or more, Mandy tried to get into the same mood Tad was already, but the pine trees flying past the window was nauseating, not exciting. Suddenly she felt her body abruptly pushed back as if it weighed practically nothing and then hurled forward just as weightlessly. She heard a scream as if in the distance but it was probably from her.

It was late June, shortly after Mandy's birthday, and the seasonable weather should have put her in a good mood. Still, she couldn't seem to get it out of her head, she needed a change in her personal life, but she didn't know what to do. It wasn't like she was eager to start dating anyone, even though she was over Tad. The problem was she wasn't over what he did to her on their wedding day.

When Mandy returned home from her midnight shift at the bakery, there was already a message on her answering machine. It was from Mrs. Mattie Douglas, whose beautiful, Federal-style house on Delaplane Avenue was the meeting place of "The Women Who Quilt Like Crazy Society." Mrs. Douglas was also the founder of the society, which she started shortly after her husband, Sherman, passed away.

After Mrs. Douglas apologized for calling so early but figured Mandy was probably still at work anyway, she went ahead and left instructions for Mandy to go to "Dee's Quilts and Crafts" on Main, to pick up a quilting project for the society to start that same day, at twelve-thirty. Mrs. Douglas briefly explained she'd received a call from Reverend John Wilkinson, regarding a lonely little girl who would benefit from a handmade quilt, "as soon as possible."

Even though Mandy usually had some breakfast and then napped for a couple hours before getting up and doing some housework, on this particular morning she didn't want to sleep. Instead she'd do some housework until it was time for Dee's to open, at ten. It seemed like it had been forever

30

since "The Women Who Quilt Like Crazy Society" convened to make a quilt for a (hopefully) grateful recipient. Some recipients were in fact so visibly depressed, a colorful quilt lifted their spirits one-hundred percent, at least while the society was making their presentation. And that often happened in a hospital room, which never failed to suffer from having even a minimum of relative hominess and comfort.

Something about the quilting project Mandy was expected to choose, made her heart go out to this little girl. Maybe it had to do with the fact Mattie Douglas mentioned the girl's father was in the hospital as well, as he had been the driver when the accident occurred. However, he was expected to be released from the hospital shortly. The girl's mother didn't drive, and she evidently wanted nothing to do with the whole situation.

This neglected girl liked animals, especially cats, and she wanted to be a veterinarian or least an assistant. Mandy appreciated the girl's aspirations; she herself always wanted to be a second-grade teacher but didn't want to bother with college because she had a hard time studying. Nevertheless, she had the discipline to show up for a job she liked, which explained how she'd lasted at Golden Crescent Bakery for over seven years.

It must have been serendipity that led to Mandy finding out about the quilting group's existence. Usually she ignored the bulletin board ads in the entryway of Plainfield's one supermarket, "Moe's." One day, she was so bored it was compelling to linger and read some of the various ads, hoping for any sort of inspiration. What caught her eye was a 4"x 6" index card with variously-colored squares around the edges. It was that and the word "crazy" within the name of the "Society." It was impressive to find so much information was very legibly printed, including the fact "a new recruit" was needed because one of the group had moved out of state to live closer to family. Also, it was preferable for the new member to have a valid driver's license and be willing "to run errands," specifically picking up quilting projects. The final request was the new volunteer liked to quilt and be in the company of others who enjoyed the pastime. Also mentioned was the fact none of the other quilters were under the age of sixty, "if that."

Mandy couldn't help smiling when reading the last part of Mrs. Douglas' ad. And she still smiled whenever she thought of it. No one in Mandy's life ever had a sense of humor, especially not Tad. Having dumped her like he did, it seemed like he'd had the last laugh.

"Dee's Quilts and Crafts" was owned by Charlotte Rufus, who ran the store, while her mother, Tina, filled in from time to time. Hopefully Charlotte was working today because Mandy wanted some help picking out the right quilting project for a lonely little girl who had done something to Mandy's heart. Finally it no longer felt irreparably broken.

The store itself was located in a red brick, flat-roofed building with a spacious second-floor apartment, which was rented out to a retired couple. Mandy wasn't sure if the Rufuses owned the building or were renters too. Neither did she know how the name "Dee" fit into the whole equation.

Mandy liked to parallel-park right in front of the building when a space was available, as there was today. Otherwise she used the parking lot behind it, reserved for the other businesses on either side and across the street from the quilting store.

Usually Mandy had the store to herself, and Charlotte would chit-chat with her from behind the counter while Mandy picked out the latest project for the quilting society. On this particular day, there were two older women going through the metal bin in the middle of the store, which was full of clearance-priced needlepoint, cross-stitch, and crewel projects.

After Charlotte and Mandy had exchanged greetings,

Mandy went in search of a suitable quilt pattern, the display of which was located in the far corner, not that the store was huge. It couldn't have been more than a thousand square feet. Typically Charlotte let Mandy browse for a couple minutes before initiating a conversation. Sometimes it was about quilting but more often it was about the weather or the latest happenings around Plainfield. Today, however, Charlotte couldn't seem to wait to ask Mandy, "So who has Mattie sent you in for, this time?"

The question sounded more pointed than usual, causing Mandy to stop and turn around before even reaching "the clearance bin." She replied, "There's a little girl who's at Saint Mercy Hospital in Toledo, and she was in a car accident with her father driving. Now Mom and Dad aren't talking, something like that. The whole thing just breaks my heart." Then she couldn't help but start crying! Mandy had considered asking Charlotte for some help picking out a project, not fall apart.

The two ladies at the bargain bin spoke right up and started to discuss the unfairness being done to "the poor little girl." Mandy recognized the one lady as a customer at the bakery. She almost mentioned something but preferred to eavesdrop; everything she heard appeared to confirm what she already knew in her heart.

"There's nothing like a new project to give us incentive," Carrie Stokes stated as the seven other members of "The Women Who Quilt Like Crazy Society" busily worked on a quilt in the dining room of Mattie Douglas' house. Everything just felt so right today, including the fact *The Toledo Enquirer* had finally realized the existence of this "society," and the ultimate tie-in was the next recipient of their latest handmade quilt. The young girl made the front page of their paper, thanks to the ditzy father, who caused the one-vehicle accident. Supposedly he wasn't even under

33

the influence of anything. Maybe he needed to give up driving, like his wife already did. Or she never drove to begin with, was how the story went. The whole family sounded weird, save for the daughter, who deserved some happiness in spite of all she'd already been put through in her short life.

Carrie didn't bother to wonder who contacted the paper, to help put the quilting society on the map; its existence relied entirely on donations, and those were usually only made after a complete quilt had been presented to its designated recipient. Because of its relative obscurity, sometimes it seemed like forever before the quilting society was back to work again. Often it was a reverend, priest, pastor, etc., who would contact them about the next quilt project, but that needed to change. It was time to update and have a website. Maybe a reality show would also help do the trick.

The Toledo Enquirer only came out on Tuesdays, so hopefully with the reporter and photographer having just arrived, they would get their story and pictures and hurry back to the office in plenty of time to complete the assignment. Since the girl receiving the quilt would only be in the hospital another forty-eight hours at the most, it seemed logical to put the quilt society's story in the paper, A.S.A.P.

The reporter from the newspaper introduced herself as Courtney Fischel and the photographer was Henry Rhodes. All the quilters briefly stopped working to say hello but couldn't wait to return to their project. The time crunch obviously inspired them.

Courtney said she would ask each one a couple questions and later a select number of responses would be chosen based on content and the space available for the article. She ended up starting her brief questioning with Mandy, who was seated closest to the door. Courtney had scribbled down each woman's name when Mattie Douglas had quickly rattled each one off. The first question for Mandy was: "How long have you been a part of this group of ladies, and what incited you to join in the first place?"

Forgetting to answer the first part of the question, Mandy replied, "I needed something new to do, as I felt like I was in a rut, personally. I'd isolated myself after enduring a huge disappointment in a serious relationship." Daring to look around, every single member of the quilting society was staring at her. Ms. Fischel was busily scribbling, looking down, and the photographer was taking pictures.

Her face feeling flushed with embarrassment, Mandy wished she would have been skipped over! It was impossible for her to keep her comments brief; she had to practically spill her guts at every opportunity, few though those were. Worse, she just realized she never answered the first part of the question – but Ms. Fischel had already moved on to the next interviewee.

Krista originally agreed to let her husband, Tad, take her to the hospital in Toledo, to shut him up. That was the reason she did most things anymore, and she'd had enough. No longer did they have a marriage but a mutual life sentence. She actually elected not to have a driver's license, mostly because her mother did the same thing, which seemed to help keep her marriage solid, although Krista couldn't say the same for hers. One problem was Tad's mother spoiled the hell out of him and made no secret of it. He was an "only child," and his mother let him take liberties for that alone.

The situation at home was a little tense right now, and Krista was doing her darndest to make sure things didn't get worse, while Tad apparently had the opposite intention. This obviously sounded like a no-win situation, so that was why Krista ended up telling her husband at the last minute, she wasn't going to the hospital after all, to pick up their daughter. It was all his fault Amanda was even there! That was a major point of contention, and it was extremely likely their marriage wouldn't survive much longer because Krista was ready to file for divorce.

Amy Kristoff

Krista had in fact already called a lawyer's office right in town, and as soon as she identified herself, the lawyer (who answered the phone) asked how Tad was, doing so in a tone of voice that indicated those two were more than mere acquaintances. Naturally the lawyer next wanted to know what Krista needed help with, and she managed to think quickly enough to reply, "I was just thinking I should make a will. Ever since having my daughter, I've had that on my mind."

"That's a wonderful idea," the lawyer replied. "Call me next week when my secretary Tracy is back from her vacation, and she can schedule a free consultation."

"Thank you," Krista said, although the lawyer had already hung up. Evidently he couldn't wait to be done with her. Was it possible Tad had already consulted with his lawyer-friend about a separation or divorce?

It was a blessing Amanda even survived the one-vehicle accident, given how Tad's beloved 2001, green Mustang convertible was crushed only on the passenger side, having clipped a utility pole on the driver's side and afterward had rolled a couple times. Tad cut his head and was knocked out, while Amanda had some bruises and scratches and was unconscious longer. Krista never would have wished outright ill on anyone, but immediately upon finding out what happened, she wished Tad had died.

As a precaution, Tad had been hospitalized for two nights, even though he maintained he was fine. After being discharged, he checked into a hotel near the hospital. Somehow he got his insurance company to pay for a rental car, so he could come and go as he pleased. Through it all, he'd made it seem like he'd gone off to war, thanks to the accident. It was infuriating how effortlessly he could put his own spin on everything, even something that should have been black and white—and consequently made him look like the selfish loser he was (although of course he didn't regard himself like that).

It just so happened Tad had the week off from work, so he had until Monday to get himself organized. Krista couldn't wait to find out where he decided to take up residence. Although she never told him as much, he was not welcome to live at home at this point, anyway. Nonetheless, she wanted the pleasure of kicking him out, versus having him simply leave. That sounded too easy on him, given the hell he'd put her through.

Since Krista didn't drive, she walked a lot and completed most of her errands without her aunt Rosalie's help. Although Krista appreciated the gesture on her aunt's part, it was more important to spend time chauffeuring Krista's mother, Gina. Even though Aunt Rosalie was only a year older than her sister, the two weren't especially close, and Krista liked to think her aunt actually enjoyed Krista's company. As it was, Aunt Rosalie never had kids, despite marrying young (and remaining happily married). Meanwhile, Krista's mother only had her and claimed to be happy about that, along with never learning how to drive a car. At this point, Krista wished she'd gotten her driver's license and had another kid. Given Tad's apparent proclivity to recklessness, it was simply being realistic, if she wanted to see at least one make it to adulthood.

Seriously, Tad and she never could have raised more than one child because they could never agree on how to raise Amanda! Krista was all for maintaining some structure to their daughter's day, even in the summer, while Tad considered complete spontaneity the best approach, year-round. Throw in a desire of his "to get back at Mom" (as he did the night he totaled his Mustang), and there was nothing productive about their disparities in raising Amanda.

On "the fateful evening," Tad couldn't wait to cave to Amanda's desire for an actual ice cream sundae, versus a frozen custard one, the latter of which was the only kind available in Jasper. An actual "ice cream parlor" was quite a drive.

The controversy had started earlier in the day, when Krista had "promised" Amanda "an ice cream" sometime following lunch. After sewing buttons back on some of Tad's shirts, Krista was so drowsy she had to lie down and take a nap. She'd intended to rest for a few minutes but ended up sleeping for more than an hour. Never before did she fall asleep at two in the afternoon, and she was infuriated with herself. Unfortunately she had to make up lost time by telling Amanda they couldn't walk up to the custard stand after all because Mommy had to start getting things ready for dinner.

Rather than nod her acceptance of as much, Amanda made a remark to the effect of being aware Krista was asleep but didn't *dare* wake her.

Upon hearing that comment, Krista got a prickly feeling on the back of her neck, just like she did when something really got to her. To think, her daughter accomplished that!

To top it off, Amanda proceeded to declare, "I wanted an ice cream anyways, not one of those swirly, custardy things that melt right away. They're hardly even cold."

Krista could hardly believe her ears. Obviously she'd been fooling herself into believing Amanda was growing into a mannerly young adult. At least Amanda's haughtiness helped Krista shake her post-nap grogginess, so she proceeded to tell her daughter, "Go to your room for the rest of the afternoon, until your father gets home and has a word with you. He wouldn't like what you just said to me, any more than I did."

After Amanda had made her slow departure down the hallway from the kitchen to her room, Krista thought about what she'd just told her daughter and realized everything might backfire. It all depended on whose "side" Tad decided to be. He was fair about matters when he would so choose, but other times he acted like objectivity was his enemy.

Either way, Amanda was acquiring quite an attitude, and her father was "the favorite parent." Naturally Amanda was copying him, most likely not even intentionally.

It sounded like a vehicle just pulled into the driveway, and a few seconds later the doorbell rang. Looking through the peephole, she saw none other than Tad. It was impossible he drove all the way to the hospital in Toledo and picked up Amanda. Having stood in the doorway and told him she wasn't going with him, Krista wasn't entirely surprised he'd returned. After all, he'd had to go out of his way to pick her up, since his hotel was near the hospital. She felt like a wimp for admitting it, but she didn't want to open the door for him. Other than his utter recklessness when driving, she didn't consider him "dangerous." That said, something about what she could decipher of his expression through a peephole, he was ready to lose it. Then again, she preferred to let him in, versus having him kick the door down. Even if he had his key, that was most likely what he'd do.

Barely did Krista turn the knob when Tad pushed the door in her face and stated, "You're coming with me to pick up Amanda. I don't give a damn what you told me a few minutes ago."

"I just need to . . ."

"I don't give half a shit what you need to do!" Tad furiously screamed. "Get in the fucking car!"

After putting on her shoes, Krista obediently left the house. This was what she got for never learning how to drive. Otherwise she could have gotten away from her maniac of a husband – provided she had a vehicle. Instead she was about to be a passenger in a car he was driving.

A habit Tad had, which Krista never could stand, was he turned to look at her while he was driving if he felt it necessary "to drive home a point." On this interminable trip to the hospital in Toledo, there'd be plenty of opportunities for that.

For the first few miles, Tad gave her the silent treatment, but once he got on the toll road, he'd start speeding and let her have it with a verbal assault. It was possible for him to take a more leisurely, two-lane route, but it wasn't in him. Krista finally dared to look at him stopped at a light, right before turning left to get on the toll road. He happened to turn his head, and his expression was eerily blank. Also, he had dark circles under his eyes, something she previously didn't notice. His pride and joy, that mop of thick, wavy, dark brown hair, was greasy – unheard of for him.

The only solace at this point was his gray Chevrolet Impala had an automatic transmission, unlike his beloved Mustang. It was just as well he'd totaled it because given the way he drove it the third clutch (or maybe even the fourth) was about to go, anyway. Krista had to giggle at that, so desperate was she for some "comic relief." Otherwise she'd start shrieking, which would only contribute to Tad's already sour mood.

With Tad in pole position, he would typically take off like he was in a race, but on this occasion he could hardly be bothered to move. He was occupied asking Krista, "What's so funny?"

"Nothing," was her reply, fully aware that response was not going to placate Tad.

"Tell me what it is," he ordered. "I could use an excuse to laugh too, right now."

Krista was not about to reveal what had triggered her giggling (which she still could barely contain), so she told him, "It's nothing, really. If I try to explain it, it'll sound even more stupid than it already is, and you won't want to laugh."

Fortunately Tad didn't care to argue, which was good; they'd already argued enough to last them the remainder of their married life, no matter how long they stayed together.

After getting his ticket at the toll plaza, Tad merged the rental car into the relatively heavy traffic without even bothering to signal. That wasn't unusual for him, and it was the least severe of his repeated examples of carelessness, which were sometimes combined with utter recklessness.

Within the next thirty seconds, Tad proceeded to end up in the innermost of three lanes, after having veered in front of and/or cut off so many vehicles, Krista lost count. She'd admittedly closed her eyes and prayed on at least two occasions.

Suddenly the car was moving much more slowly, and Krista realized she must have closed her eyes yet again, but this time it was only for a few seconds. In front of Tad's rental, there was a white Oldsmobile Ciera. Its driver was half-heartedly attempting to pass an eighteen-wheeler in the middle lane. At this rate it would take a couple miles for the Ciera driver to finish passing the truck.

Tad's impatient response to the situation was to slow down even more and proceed to dodge behind the tractor-trailer and then cut someone off in the far right lane. He was rewarded for as much by being loudly honked at, causing him to smile. Despite the circumstances it was a relief to see him do that, versus having him look like a zombie.

There was about a hundred-yard gap between Tad's rental car and the next vehicle in the far right lane, and he was determined to get behind that vehicle as quickly as possible. Meanwhile, the middle lane was a solid line of cars, trucks and tractor-trailers, so he was pretty much stuck in this lane until it was time to exit.

Krista vowed not to be a coward and close her eyes anymore because Tad's reckless driving was building a case for her when they divorced. In other words, she could potentially get full custody of Amanda if it could be proven Tad shouldn't be trusted with their daughter, especially whenever he was behind the wheel.

That idea made Krista wonder: was it possible Tad could have had criminal charges filed against him after his latest mishap? It appeared to work to his advantage, his beloved Mustang was the only vehicle involved in the accident. The police investigation was minimal, and there was no insurance claim besides his own.

41

By this time Tad was relentlessly tail gaiting the older, tan Buick sedan that was in the far right lane, with numerous vehicles ahead of it. Traffic in the right lane was closing the gap with the rental car both in front of and behind it, so there really was nothing for Tad to do but stay where he was until it was time to exit. There was no better time to open the lines of communication, as he finally had no choice but to listen. It was surprising he hadn't started a diatribe himself, at this point.

Krista began by bluntly stating, "I want to let you know I intend to file for divorce as soon as I find a lawyer."

The second Tad heard that, he burst into laughter and sounded like he'd never be able to stop. At least he got his opportunity to laugh. After finally getting his emotions under control he declared, "I just love what you told me. You couldn't have done a better job of making me laugh if you'd tried."

"What's so funny about what I said?" Krista wanted to know. "I was just giving you fair warning because you should have that."

"Gee. Thanks," Tad remarked and proceeded to slam on the brakes, as the Buick he kept tail gaiting, abruptly slowed down. Teeth gritted, he added, "Thanks as well for distracting me to the point I can't drive. I could have hit that idiot in front of me."

Rather than apologize (why bother?) Krista muttered, "You can't drive anyway. So what?"

"Excuse me?" Tad asked, his interest piqued to the point he not only turned to look at her but abruptly hit the brakes again, after having briefly accelerated.

Krista glanced in the passenger-side rearview mirror and witnessed an older, white Chevrolet pick-up, pulling over to the shoulder. Its brakes probably went out, thanks to Tad. He had no right to blame her for what he did behind the wheel. There was in fact a rumor he almost killed a woman he'd been engaged to while he was still in college, but he

ended up breaking up with her because his dear mother did-n't like the young woman.

Tad had somehow remembered to start moving again, but he remained more interested in Krista; in other words he was staring at her. She hadn't noticed because she kept looking in the rearview mirror. It was just as well; the look he was giving her was absolutely chilling. In the meantime, the Buick that Tad had tail gaited was long gone for whatever reason. The driver might have exited the expressway but most probably left Tad in the dust.

"I asked you a question, Krista," Tad finally said.

"I missed it. I'm sorry," she told him.

"I excused myself and made it a question," Tad stated, barely able to contain his irritation. "You were supposed to consider it a request for a repeat of what you'd just said. Do you follow me?"

"No, not really," Krista admitted, getting flustered. It was more than apparent Tad was extremely upset, given his clenched jaw. With him behind the wheel of a car, she could-n't imagine how this scenario would play out. At least Amanda wasn't with them this time.

Daring to look ahead, Krista noticed there wasn't a vehi-cle in the far right lane for several dozen yards, maybe more. Even though their car had to be going at least fifty m.p.h. at this point, it was being passed on the left as if Tad were bare-ly pushing the gas pedal. He said, "I saw someone today, I hadn't expected to meet again. I wish I could have had the heart to tell her how sorry I am. I'm just realizing that."

About a third of a mile ahead, there was an overpass. Krista's line of sight zeroed in on its concrete posts on the right side, even though they temporarily remained in the dis-tance.

As if to fuel her apprehension, Tad suddenly floored the gas pedal. The only "good news" was he was looking in the direction they were traveling.

Tad proceeded to slam the Impala into the far right side

43

of the viaduct, careful not to involve any other vehicles in the collision. With that he was successful.

Happily Ever After—for Whom?

Warren Kensit had a lot to prove to his super-hot, latest girlfriend, Toni Walkins. Thirty-ish like himself, she didn't have any kids but did have two ex-husbands to her credit. Warren refused to see the latter as a red flag and in the meantime was falling in love with her. There was an obvious problem with that: Toni and he had yet to consummate their relationship. They had nonetheless shared plenty of make-out sessions, and Warren had no doubt she could sexually satisfy him "for the duration." In other words he could imagine marrying her and never getting tired of waking up next to her hot body. Having dated her for close to seven weeks, he couldn't help hinting to her about ten days earlier, on the way to dinner, it was "about time to take things to the next level." Hopeless romantic though he was, it was impossible to sound like anything but a single-minded moron when he was trying to make his case but not appear anxious.

It must be mentioned, Warren wasn't expected to pick up the check every time Toni and he went out. Usually they "took turns," but for the last couple dates, Toni had insisted on paying. That included the date on which beforehand he'd dropped his "obvious hint." They'd been on their way to "The Other Place," on Lincoln Road, in Scottsdale, Arizona. It was a unique but also quite a pricey dining destination, yet Toni was absolutely insistent about paying the bill. He'd dared to think perhaps she finally wanted to go back to his condo, something she kept mentioning. Otherwise, he'd take her back to her tan stucco, red-tile roofed bungalow (in a cookie-cutter subdivision), and they'd kiss on the front stoop. There was always plenty of passion, including from her, and she never failed to say, "I can't wait to see you again."

Not too surprisingly, Toni ended up doing the usual, after the date. Also, she wasn't heard from for several days, which wasn't atypical, either. Times like these were when Warren wondered how exclusive their relationship was. The bottom line: he was very frustrated, especially when considering the possibility she was seeing someone else and on an intimate level. He hated that.

The Fourth of July fell on a Saturday, so Warren had planned on sleeping in and going to a casino later in the day. Out of the blue, Toni called about nine-thirty, with a rather strange request. Naturally Warren couldn't wait to agree to it.

This sure as hell was turning out to be a completely different Fourth of July from what Warren had in mind. That said, it wasn't as if he'd wanted to go to the casino, alone. However, at the end of their last date, besides being given the send-off yet again, he'd been forewarned Toni was "completely busy" the entire Fourth of July weekend, as if letting him know not to bother calling her, even to say "hi."

It was barely eleven A.M., the sun was already blazing hot, and Warren was about to hit his first practice shot at the driving range of semi-private "Tierra Verde Country Club." This was the last place he'd expected to be, especially at Toni's beckoning. Just for that, he needed to take a couple more practice swings before hitting the first shot, using the driver, his favorite club.

As mentioned, Toni had called earlier this morning, to ask him if he cared to meet her at Tierra Verde, all so she could watch him hit a bucket of balls at the driving range. She was already aware of his fondness for hitting balls, but it was nonetheless unbelievable she would suggest they meet so she could witness him do so, especially on a hot summer's day. Fortunately for Toni, there was a wooden bench under a large mesquite tree, right behind where Warren had teed up his first shot. To make sure no unwanted ultraviolet rays hit Toni's gorgeous face, she was wearing a red straw, wide-brimmed hat, which matched her red, purple, and turquoise (with a white background), polka-dot sundress. Despite the heat, her wavy, shoulder-length, dark brown hair hung loose. She looked like a model in a magazine ad.

For the time being, Warren just wanted to impress Toni, although doing so would be a tall order. He took one more practice swing before finally hitting the first ball. If he missed it because he "looked up," it was doubtful she would have any idea and would assume he'd taken another practice swing.

It turned out the first shot was pretty good, sailing about 175 yards. If Warren kept moving things along, keeping Toni's attention wouldn't become a problem. He'd intended to only get a small bucket of balls but stupidly got a large bucket. He'd simply have to leave the unused balls here, which he hated to do. What he liked was to offer any remaining balls to a fellow driving range attendee. Obviously this was one morning when he had the place to himself. However, there were a few golfers braving the heat to play nine or eighteen holes.

After hitting a couple more shots with his driver, each one going further than the one before it, Warren expected Toni to compliment him but she didn't say a word. He refused to feel daunted and would stick with this club until he nailed a few. Then Toni would have no choice but to ooh and ah.

Finally Warren needed a new tee, but he didn't have any on him, other than the one he just broke. So he did the usual and looked around for one. That was when he caught a glimpse of Toni, literally running toward the clubhouse/pro shop. The second story, where the pro shop was located, was accessible directly from the driving range, which overlooked pretty much everything, including the parking lot, behind it.

Rather than wonder what the hell Toni might be up to, Warren vowed to remain unconcerned (even though he contemplated her possible inner thoughts practically every second, when he was with her). Most likely she went in search of a restroom, was all. She was definitely a private person.

Having located a tee, Warren decided to change clubs and would save the tee for later. He'd hit a few balls with his three-iron, a club he tended to have trouble with. Admittedly he could hardly concentrate, knowing Toni suddenly left, making no mention of where she was going. He just revealed how she was a private person and all that, but something didn't seem right. If nothing else she decided to ditch him.

That possibility compelled Warren to drop his three-iron (after having "looked up"), and he jogged in the same direction Toni went. On the way, he couldn't help noticing two people on the balcony outside the pro shop. They were surveying the course. In this heat? Warren wondered. One last glance, and he swore the man was his boss, Hamilton Sinclair. Suddenly everything seemed very confusing, even though nothing had yet "happened." It was a known fact Hamilton was supposedly "happily married" yet had a girlfriend. Meanwhile, Warren knew next to nothing about Toni, other than she was twice-divorced and had no children. She didn't have a job because she didn't need to work, intimating she had always been wealthy. However, most likely she had her two exes to thank.

Something was up. A woman like Toni didn't do anything without a motive, which gave her ongoing impetus. Relaxing for a minute would kill her. As it was, Warren was in way over his head. Still, he would go in pursuit of her in a minute; he didn't want to look like he was worried about possibly being dumped.

When Toni Walkins had a definite plan, there'd better not be anyone to get in her way. If he did, one way or another, he would be sorry. As for this Warren-guy she'd been dating, he was a real find but not in the conventional sense of the word. At the same time, he admittedly was a nice guy -- but she liked challenges, damn it! Anyway, she needed to exact some revenge on a married man she'd mindlessly had an affair with, having assumed he was going to leave his wife. His nerve was what burned her up the most. Not only that, he was probably worth more than both her ex-husbands, combined. "Mr. Right" broke things off as recently as very early this morning, explaining he was "happily married and wanted to stay that way." He told her that as a farewell, yet she not only couldn't find it in herself to be offended, she kept calling his cell phone, desperate to work things out. He finally answered, shortly before she came to "Tierra Verde Country Club," essentially to spy on him. He'd told her he would be stopping here to look it over as a place for "a cele-bration," whatever the hell that meant. Obviously he wasn't referring to their wedding reception, once he'd divorced his wife. Toni had asked him why he wanted to end things so abruptly, to which he'd replied, "I'd told Mandra I was going on an overnight golfing trip with a couple golf buddies, to Tucson. I woke up next to you, and I hated myself for it! Mandra doesn't deserve to be outright lied to. That's ridicu-lous!"

Toni could not stress it enough, she did not accept rejec-tion and just walk away. In this particular situation, the only permissible ending was the one *she* created. She'd evi-dently made a huge mistake by thinking she could get "Ham"(formally Hamilton) to fall madly in love with her or whatever the hell men did, who had everything but threw it away to marry someone like her. Ham already "stepped in it" by having an affair, so he couldn't have been too worried about losing the respect of his wife and three daughters, not to mention losing plenty of money and assets, should

Amy Kristoff

Mandra come to her senses and divorce him.

Warren Kensit was an employee of Ham's, or none of this would have been possible. And it shouldn't have been, only because Warren was completely capable of running his own business. Although Toni never slept with Warren, she felt like she could assess his business acumen, and he had Ham beat by a mile. Maybe she'd run into Warren in a few years, and if she hadn't found her third and final "Mr. Right" . . .

It came in handy Ham had brought her to this country club for lunch on a few occasions. Even though he didn't have a residence within the perimeters of the Tierra Verde Country Club developments, he had a golf membership and apparently couldn't get enough of the place. Or maybe his wife detested it so he figured it was safe to bring Toni here.

Toni had to pass through the pro shop in order to reach the balcony where Ham was standing next to a young-look-ing (barely legal), tall, exceptionally attractive brunette. It was convenient to take this route because she could grab a weapon. Otherwise she'd intended to strangle her ex-lover, figuring she was angry enough to pull it off. Besides, Ham would be too shocked to resist. Meanwhile, his "other girl-friend" would be too mortified to do anything but stand there in her short, white denim jeans shorts and a hot pink tank top. Given how she filled out that top but was tall and thin (given what Toni could see of her), it was a safe bet she'd had plastic surgery.

There was a row of putters in the far right corner of the pro shop, as Toni had entered via the glass doors on the east side. There was also a putting green in the corner, obviously for trying out a new putter. How convenient—except she had another way to try one out. She didn't give a shit about the game of golf anyway. What a bore! Seeking revenge was much more exciting.

Grabbing the closest putter, only once Toni ditched her stupid hat did she realize she'd picked one that resembled an actual club more so than a stream-lined putter. The blonde behind the counter was so busy yapping on the phone, she didn't even notice Toni breeze right past her with the clunky putter and open the oversized French door leading to the patio. Meanwhile, Ham had his arm around his "new" lover, as the two continued to take in the view of several golf holes, the fairways flanked by impressively-large, Mediterranean-style houses on the left and one-story, flat-roofed, tan stucco condominiums on the right. If only Ham had purchased one of those quasi-mansions, his long-suffering wife could have witnessed her husband and his lover get literally whacked, provided Mandra had a pair of binoculars.

As Ham and his underage girlfriend continued to dawdle, entirely oblivious to Toni's presence, she raised her arms, preparing to hit them both. Not two seconds later, her arms were forced against her sides, causing her to react by emitting a yelp of surprise.

Toni's exclamation finally forced Hamilton out of his reflective state and he turned around, in sync with his new girlfriend or whatever the hell she was supposed to be. By the way, who could have possibly stopped Toni from completing her mission? The first person who came to mind was one of the assistant pros who managed to be around whenever a golf course was open, even on a scorching-hot day. She didn't mind at all, one of them might have his body close to hers. It wasn't possible Warren had any idea what she was up to. No way. She was too clever. But admittedly he was a nice guy.

Hamilton was standing on the balcony of Tierra Verde Country Club's pro shop with his youngest daughter, Tiffany. Having recently graduated from high school, she managed to eff-up her future by getting pregnant. Not only that, she wasn't sure if she wanted to marry the guy, Daniel, despite his "earnest" marriage proposal, thanks to pressure from his parents. As it was, Hamilton and his wife, Mandra, were all for Daniel's effort "to do the right thing."

Having brought Tiffany to the country club, attempting to "sell her" on the idea of having the wedding reception here, Hamilton fully expected his youngest (of three) daughters to finally tell her boyfriend she would accept his proposal. If she inquired about any other options, Hamilton was prepared to calmly tell her she would be disowned. Mandra had no clue he intended to use this tactic; instead, before leaving the house, he'd assured her he'd "get it done." Since he'd spent the night "away" and only showed up long enough to pick up Tiffany, Hamilton was spared from having to go into a long discussion about anything. After this, Tiffany and he were headed to a barbecue hosted by a close family friend. Fortunately no relatives would be there, just his wife and their two other daughters, Paula and Celine. Fortunately they knew not to ask about any family issues, unless their father brought them up first.

Tiffany was always rebellious, at least compared to her older sisters, both of whom were very self-possessed and responsible. If Tiffany found out she'd be disowned and disinherited for continuing to be rebellious, she'd marry Daniel and live happily ever after.

Just as Hamilton about had his fill of enduring the late-morning heat of Scottsdale on the Fourth of July, noticeable even in the shade, behind him there was a sudden, strange-sounding cry, followed by some arguing between a couple. Hamilton'd had his arm around Tiffany, as they were both gazing at the front-nine layout of two eighteen-hole courses. Most casual visitors had no idea there were two courses here. Anyway, if Tiffany's wedding reception took place by September 30th, Hamilton would save a whole hell of a lot of money. After the golf season starting picking back up, the fee to close this place down for a few hours, would double.

Hamilton made the mistake of turning around, witnessing none other than his ex-lover, Toni Walkins, being "subdued" by none other than his best employee ever, Warren

Kensit. If Kensit's work ethic followed his dating proclivities, it was not a straight line from one to the other. In other words, what the hell was he doing with a money-grubbing skank like Toni? Then again, it was possible he'd simply been in the pro shop and came to the rescue. Now that sounded more like him.

For the time being, Hamilton pretended not to know his ex-lover, Toni, as they had broken up earlier in the day. He'd lied to his wife about where he was last night, all so he could be with a woman he never should have met. Enough was enough.

"Warren Kensit, what brings you here?" Hamilton asked, starting down his road of "elective amnesia." The subsequent look Warren gave him, indicated he already figured something was up between his boss and the hellion, Toni. Meanwhile, Warren had done an absolutely admirable job of continuing to subdue her, as she'd made every effort to use none other than a putter to "club" Hamilton and Tiffany. It was unbelievable yet not entirely surprising, given her temperament.

Before Warren had a chance to reply, Hamilton's daughter asked him, sounding as if the reply was important, "Daddy how do you know this Warren-guy? Does he work at your company?"

"Yes, darling, he does," Hamilton quickly replied, preoccupied with this entire situation and how it would continue to unfold.

A second later, Tiffany stepped forward and proceeded to shake hands with Warren! In the meantime, Warren had taken full possession of the putter Toni had intended to use as a weapon. He was holding it with his free hand while Tiffany started giddily talking to him a mile a minute about God only knew what. It was impossible for Hamilton to decipher what she was saying, not only because she was talking too fast and had her back to him, but he was starting to think perhaps this whole experience was a figment of his imagination.

At this point there was nothing for Hamilton to do but let Tiffany "follow her heart" and get to know Warren Kensit. Her eighteen to his thirty-two or three? That really wasn't too much of an age discrepancy, once the inevitability started to sink in.

As Toni winked at Hamilton and discreetly left, he realized he'd just been dug out of a huge hole, by his pregnant, teenaged daughter! How many philandering fathers could have ever made such a declaration?

The Secret Gourmet

My husband managed to put up a good front, in more ways than one. It was that or lose his dream job, not only because of the pay but the fringe benefits. Also, there was nothing like making a very good living at doing what you loved best.

How Marcus and I met could have been the plot for a feel-good love story (about eccentrics). I was a cashier making eleven bucks an hour at the Scottsdale, Arizona location of independently-owned "Sammy's Supermarket." Meanwhile, Marcus regularly stopped in the store but somehow never did so when I was working. Either that or he never ended up using my register to check out. It was a big store with several cashiers on duty from opening until closing, seven days a week.

Verne Stockton was the store manager who was usually working when I was and he couldn't stand me. If I hadn't liked where I was employed, I would have found another place to be a cashier. Having been hired by the head manager, Mr. Passel, I was practically literally a thorn in Verne's side. He tried to make me miserable, hoping I would quit. I'd lasted six months so far, and I was getting better and better at tolerating his short temper and hyper-criticism as well as his lingering looks—never of approval, of course.

Marcus had a confidentiality agreement with his boss, while I had my own sort of "secret": I was obsessed with scanning items. It was therapeutic to move an object over a sensor and hear the "beep." That was the kind of thing a

Amy Kristoff

never-married, thirty-seven-year-old, reasonably attractive woman could get into, especially if she had no interests and her relationships were few and far between. Through it all, I never failed to hold out hope I'd eventually marry, despite my pessimistic mother, having written me off as a hopeless spinster. She lived in Flagstaff, spending her days lamenting she should have had one more kid, to increase her chances of having a grandchild before it was "too late." I assumed that referred to her chances of living long enough to see the much-anticipated grandchild. Otherwise, she had my demise in mind. Mother did have a creepy aura, despite her still-stunning looks at 69. My father committed suicide when they were both sixty-two. At least, that was how he supposedly passed, as he had been quite ill. Meanwhile, Mother refused to talk about the circumstances surrounding Dad's death. Until he became sick, he always had such a zest for life, unlike Mother, who was miserable for as long as I remembered. It was one reason of many I'd kept my distance as an adult.

Marcus was forty-two when we met, making him the perfect "older man," without being old. He'd never married either, which helped him avoid the inevitable cynicism toward marriage, which crept in for an individual who had gone through a bitter divorce or two. Like myself as well, he had no children, which made our getting-to-know-each-other phase much more enjoyable. It didn't take long for me to be the envy of any female co-workers younger than me but already married with kids.

What had initially drawn me to Marcus was his unabashed enthusiasm for life, which reminded me of my father, what little time we'd spent together over the years. He was seemingly always on the road, working as a truck driver. I couldn't blame him for wanting to stay away.

And Marcus' pick-up line was so bold, it was hard to

resist (but I did at first, only to make him "want me more"). Besides, it was impossible to completely blow him off when I was instantaneously attracted to him. It was love at first sight, something I never believed in until that moment.

Marcus had made a beeline for the check stand I was at on this fateful morning, number seven. I'd just finished scanning a large order, so I was relatively relaxed. Otherwise, when I had my initial exchange with Marcus, I would have forgotten to scan any items and would have stood there chatting, instead. Obviously my obsession with scanning items didn't override the effect of "love at first sight."

Not to make excuses for myself, but that was why I immediately said, "Sure," when asked by him, "I'd like to take you to dinner, preferably tonight about eight?"

Given the items Marcus purchased, I came up negative regarding what type of guy he was, other than a healthily eating and drinking (including alcohol) man, perhaps with a wife or girlfriend – or maybe not. Or he had both! All I knew was I didn't see a wedding band, not that it meant anything. It was possible to lose my mind, considering the possibilities! At least I possessed the wherewithal to tell him we'd have to meet at his restaurant of choice, versus having him pick me up. Wasn't it bad enough he knew where I worked?

Only while driving home at three-thirty did the whole "dinner date with a complete stranger" seem like an absolutely insane idea. I couldn't wait.

"Chez Milo" was the restaurant Marcus chose, and that right there meant he was "serious." It happened to be located close to where I lived but was way out of my price range. I'd only agreed to meet him after being repeatedly told my meal would be paid for. Once I'd been won over, Marcus added, "Milo and I are good friends, so he'll be sure to give me a good deal."

A *good deal*? That was all I could think, following the strange remark. It was impressive to find out Marcus knew the esteemed Milo, but were we only going there so Marcus could impress me at a discount? That sounded so cheap! (I always did have a tendency to overvalue myself.)

At home, a new problem loomed: there wasn't a single thing to wear. Naturally it wasn't for lack of clothes. But I didn't want to go out looking for a new outfit, only to end up wondering why the hell I'd looked forward to going out with this guy! I reminded myself one last time, I didn't have to go through with this dinner date. Marcus had even given me his cell phone number, should something come up. I never gave him any phone numbers, so I as good as acted as if I would show up no matter what. He was probably laughing at how gullible I was. He couldn't wait to decapitate me upon my arrival in a new, white, Volkswagen GTI. The blood spatters on the tan leather interior would never clean up. My pride and joy as of late was this car because it was the first brand-new one I'd ever purchased, and it was fun to drive. It wasn't like it was a head-turner, but I wasn't much for being noticed, anyway.

Since I was having some last-minute misgivings, it was time to call my mother in Flagstaff and tell her I was going on a date I wasn't sure about and . . . No, that wouldn't work. We weren't even close, and I hadn't spoken with her since I couldn't remember. She'd leap at the chance to chastise me for being so reckless. For a change, I would have had to agree.

I had a couple girlfriends I'd known since high school, but I wasn't close enough to either one, to call and say I needed someone "to check in with" at the end of the evening.

That sounded terrible – and ridiculous! Nothing awful could possibly take place because I was asking for so little at this point: to return home intact! At the same time, I really did think Marcus was "The One." So despite my obvious ambivalence, I was willing to accept a marriage proposal.

The much-anticipated first date with Marcus at Chez

Milo turned out to be anticlimactic, which was only my opinion. I must have expected to be wined, dined, and swept off my feet, but I only got the first two. There wasn't even a good-night kiss!

Probably the worst part was we not only sat near the kitchen but at the end of a seemingly very long, oak booth with a high back. There was a pastel-colored, paisley print on the off-white cotton fabric, and the five individual tables for two had maroon linen tablecloths. Oak wooden, round-backed chairs faced the bench, the table at each end having two chairs instead of one (as well as larger tables). This seating arrangement did not provide a personable dining experience, especially thanks to the older couple sitting at the table to Marcus' and my right, despite the fact we were seated at one end of the tables for four and had left the two places closest to the couple, vacant. One good part was the "subdued" lighting.

I started to feel as if I'd need to be subdued if the old biddy didn't quit staring at me. What the hell was her problem? Did I resemble her daughter, had she lived to be my age? That sounded morbid, but it was the conclusion I was stuck on, waiting for the first round of drinks. Marcus had been quite aggressive when requesting a dinner date, but he had become almost withdrawn. I hoped the vodka martini he'd ordered, brought him out of his shell, because I was no conversationalist.

The couple to our right wasn't interested in any small talk; they looked old enough to be in the category of: "It's All Been Said." Most everyone else were yapping away, apparently competing for the opportunity to be heard by their dining companion(s). It sounded almost like a dining hall. And I'd made the mistake of relegating Marcus to "the bench," while "the staring old lady" happened to be sitting near him, giving her an unobstructed view of me. The kitchen was to our left, so that didn't help matters either, as far as how impersonal the restaurant felt.

Only later did Marcus confess why he was suddenly so reticent on our first date: I looked so ravishing he was speechless. I was flattered, having been told as much, but he'd revealed his feelings long after the fact (we were married by then).

At this particular point in time, I'd started to wonder if I'd gotten my hopes needlessly up. I hurriedly downed my first gin and tonic, expecting to immediately relax and enjoy the environment. I figured there was no ditching him early because he knew where I worked and could track me down. Just kidding—sort of.

The "first date" would turn out to be one of many. In other words, Marcus continued to wine and dine me, insisting upon paying the bill at various upscale restaurants in the Phoenix valley. It didn't take long to cease being suspicious he had some sort of ulterior motive, whether it be bedding me or murdering me. It appeared these dining establishments we frequented were the point of us being together, as in he was a food critic in addition to his purported career as a "personal cook and nutrition consultant." That was the extent of his elaborating.

At the very end of that first date, I was more than ready for a good night kiss. After all, the evening hadn't been exactly enjoyable, not that anything was Marcus' fault, other than him not being talkative. I'd believed him when he said he knew Milo, but I wasn't permitted to meet him because Marcus didn't like to bother anyone at work. We'd just left the restaurant when he told me that; if I had the nerve, I would have called him a hypocrite.

Even a brief hug would have been better than nothing, and it wouldn't have bothered me at all to share this embrace right in the parking lot of Chez Milo. It was private, compared to the restaurant itself.

Marcus proceeded to escort me halfway to my car and

exclaimed, "See you at Sammy's tomorrow morning!" Then he turned and literally ran away!

In reply, all I could muster was, "O.K. Thanks for dinner." He probably didn't even hear me, given his big hurry. However, he did know I was working the following day, as I'd written down my hours on a cocktail napkin. And I was looking forward to seeing him again.

I started work at eight Friday morning, which was typically a pretty busy day, but it usually didn't get hectic until around noon. This particular Friday got busy by nine. Two more cashiers weren't due in before eleven, and Verne was frustrated he couldn't get ahold of either one, to tell them to come in early. Politely making the same request wasn't in him. I was glad to already be working, or I would have gotten one of his phone calls, even if I wasn't scheduled to come in at all. The handful of times he'd "told me" to come in yet I was off the whole day, I did so. It didn't occur to me to say no because I never had anything else to do!

Again I happened to be working at check stand number seven, the same place I'd been when Marcus had asked me out the day before. My first break was cut in half because Verne had asked me to return from the restroom and rather than go outside, return to my check stand. It was already that busy. Obviously it pained him to need me, but it was that or he'd have to open a register, himself. It would possibly come to that, anyway.

Marcus made his appearance about twenty minutes after my break, and things were getting more and more hectic. Determined to use my check stand, he had to wait behind four customers, one of whom was unloading a very large order. Fortunately I had help bagging, from a courtesy clerk I'd never seen before, which wasn't surprising, given the turn over rate here—largely thanks to Verne.

Check stand six to my right and number eight to my left

Amy Kristoff

had both been closed, but Barb, a part-time cashier, appeared at number eight. She said, "I'll take whoever's next in line," referring to my check stand. The customer darted over but only had about thirty items, so the customer behind her followed, logically figuring it would be faster than waiting behind the customer with the large order.

What all this came down to was Marcus was next in line and appeared very eager to see me. The second he caught my eye (I'd been attempting to be coy but could hardly keep from looking at him), he said, "Good morning, Elsa. Wonderful to see you again."

"Thank you," I responded, which sounded completely stupid. I wasn't prepared for how formal he sounded. Was he trying to "undo me," or did he have some other motive? I barely knew him at this point, so I had little to go on.

Then I spied Verne. Things were still backed up, so he logically should have opened a register, despite his aversion to doing so. In this case, he was concerned about me having exchanged a few words with "a customer." If only he'd had any idea.

Verne edged up next to me and whispered, "You know the rule about not making small-talk with customers, whether or not you know them." He started to leave before turning back around to add, "And that rule violation is double if you insist upon yakking with a customer who isn't even first in line." He was hissing like a snake before finishing his little rant.

"I beg your pardon?" Marcus loudly asked, just as I finished the transaction of the customer ahead of him. It was plain he heard Verne just fine, since he'd already unloaded his cart and had nothing better to do than eavesdrop. As it was, Verne wasn't whispering by the time he was done.

Suddenly there was an override needed on check stand two, and I had already started scanning Marcus' order, which began with two bottles of wine I'd never before seen. A price-check was in order unless Verne knew what the price was.

"Thirty-one ninety-nine a bottle," Verne said, noticing there were two. "My wife loves to drink that, but it's saved for special occasions."

"I have the afternoon and evening off," Marcus said, catching my eye, "and I'd like to invite you over to my place for dinner. I'm not the greatest cook, but I like to think I can make a meal pretty damned tasty while it's also low-calorie. Will you accept?"

"Yes, of course," I replied, forgetting I still hardly knew this man. Obviously I was unable to resist him. Now I was going to his house *and* intended to eat dinner with him, something he would be preparing. I couldn't wait.

While Verne should have been long gone, he ended up sticking around. Also, I had yet to add the two bottles of wine to Marcus' order. Just as I started entering the price on the register, Verne said, "You can have the two bottles of wine on me if you can get Elsa to leave. I've had enough of her."

My body froze when I heard that. It was extremely demeaning to be complained about as if I was incompetent! I told Verne, "I'll tell you right now, I quit . . . after I finish Marcus' order."

"Good for you, Elsa," Marcus said. "You don't need this job anyway. I'll take care of you."

Nodding at me, Verne said, "Congratulations. You not only got me out of having to pay your unemployment, I think you have a marriage proposal on your hands. I think that should add up to just one bottle on me and you pay for the other bottle."

I was suddenly more happy than ever to quit – and Marcus got two free bottles of wine. If Verne wanted to charge me for one, he could deduct it from my final pay check. In the meantime I also scanned the groceries for the customer behind Marcus, only because she'd patiently waited through all the drama. By the time I was ready to leave "for good," Verne was nowhere to be seen, which was fine with me.

As mentioned, I "dated" Marcus for two months, being wined and dined, while I suspected he was a food critic, for extra income. Since I'd lost my job, naturally I kept going along with him, especially since he'd claimed in Sammy's, that he'd take care of me. Of course I neither wanted nor expected Marcus to do so, even after going to his house for dinner. He'd proposed a toast to me quitting, and I was congratulated for my "independent spirit." After clinking our wine glasses, we polished off one of his "free" bottles of wine.

The positively delicious, five-course meal was memorable, as much as the view offered from the floor-to-ceiling, dining room windows of his house. It was nestled about halfway up Mummy Mountain. Even though it was only one-story, it had to be 4,000 square feet, with granite tile and wood floors throughout, other than the guest bedroom and bathroom. At some point between courses, Marcus mentioned his boss lived in a similar-looking, Mediterranean-style house, "much bigger and even higher up on the mountain." I considered it rather odd, the way he'd worded that statement. Also, the tone in his voice was detached, indicating he possibly rented this house, versus being the owner. Either way, Marcus made a very good living as a "personal cook and nutrition consultant." Apparently my full stomach made me feel satisfied with the information I'd been given. In the back of my mind, however, I had a feeling some of it was too good to be true.

Obediently leaving Marcus' around ten, arrangements were already in place for him to pick me up at my place the next evening around six-thirty. I hadn't received a kiss or even a hug before departing, yet it didn't seem to phase me. And I was too traditional "to make the first move."

Actually making my departure was not that simple, as I

had to descend a steep, narrow, paved driveway that had no lighting. Doing so was very disorienting, not only because of the potential danger but the fact I drank too much wine. Also, I was completely baffled by this "new person" in my life, who made no secret of wanting to share his life with me but didn't care to reveal much. The most bothersome aspect was his apparent sworn oath to secrecy – and my acceptance of as much.

Eventually I gained a few pounds, which was inevitable because I had little to do all day but wait to go out to dinner again. We only went out a couple times a week (a third time if he had the evening off), but since I'd never dined at any upscale restaurants before meeting Marcus, it seemed like we went out to dinner every night. What I needed was for him to cook some more "low-calorie" dinners at home, although obviously he didn't especially want to cook much when he had some free time.

In the meantime, I did little to find "new employment." I kept dragging my feet because I figured no sane employer would believe me if I told him or her I quit due to my boss hating me. By no means was I waiting for Marcus to finally take me up on his offer to "take care of me." I just wanted him to make a pass, but I was giving up hope.

The night before yet another "dinner date" with Marcus, I finally did the unthinkable and called my mother, not intending to outright ask for some personal advice but would do so if chatting with her didn't become uncomfortable (like it usually did after about two minutes, tops).

Whatever the cause, I suddenly felt more at ease talking to (and listening to) my mother than ever before. Maybe I was finally desperate for someone to confide in, and despite everything, it came back to her. I ended up telling her more of "my situation" with Marcus than I'd intended to, but she was her typically pragmatic self and advised me to outright tell him at the end of the date, exactly how I felt (frustrated and confused). That was my plan of action should he continue to fail to make some sort of sexual advance. My mother's final comment was: "Believe it or not, there are a few men out there, too polite to appear what they consider 'aggressive.' And for them, it doesn't take much to feel like they fill that description."

Already it'd been five years since Marcus "swept me off my feet" and continued to do so. The proof was the fact I still didn't know exactly what he did for a living – other than what he'd repeatedly told me. There had to be much more to the story, but I'd purposely made a lame effort getting any details. I truly was the obedient wife and evidently proud of as much. I never even bothered to wonder why Marcus would seem so frustrated sometimes "after returning home from work." What could have been so awful about his boss? The guy lived a couple hundred yards away, making the commute a breeze! Then again, I should have known as well as anyone, the situation with a boss often times was not what it seemed.

I not only married Marcus, I managed to gain about ten pounds by our wedding day. Worse, I gained another ten in the duration. And I did more of the cooking than Marcus, so the "low-calorie meals" were few and far between. Even more pathetic was the fact I didn't care I'd gained weight and was completely happy doing little more all day than keeping the house clean. I didn't even miss not scanning anything! Obviously I wasn't as obsessed with it as I'd thought.

Marcus and I no longer went out to dinner more than a couple times a month. However, he did like to throw cocktail and dinner parties, especially as of late. His boss had taken to demanding more and more of Marcus' time and contacted him on a whim – often late at night. There must have been something in a new contract Marcus signed, stipulating he be available 24/7, to cook for his boss. The salary increase must have been worth it, yet Marcus seemed to be more miserable than ever. He even once muttered, "I am really going to lose it soon," but he wasn't aware I heard.

The fact Marcus was "on call" didn't bother me at all, as I was a homebody. Through it all, I had my mother to thank for keeping us together. I'd used her advice and when Marcus heard me out, he playfully replied, "If I'd known that, I would have quit taking you out! I'd wanted to tell you how I felt, but I feared coming off sounding like an intrusive dope. Then the longer I waited, the harder it became to do something. I figured as long as I kept taking you out, at least hopefully you'd stick around."

Having opened my big mouth, I'd ended up spending the night at his place, and it was definitely a passionate time. Neither one of us had been in a serious relationship for a while, had never married nor had any kids . . . Maybe we both should have been at least slightly wary, but as for myself, I threw all caution to the wind.

Needless to say, we couldn't wait to get married. Misery loves company, right? Seriously, we finally had a chance to "really talk" and realized we had a lot in common, particularly the same general outlook. Or so it appeared. At least he agreed to keep the wedding intimate, to the point we took care of all the legal issues with no one but anonymous witnesses present, and we went out to dinner for the finale. My mother didn't even find out until after the fact, which she didn't take offense to and was relieved not to have to bother to drive to Phoenix from Flagstaff, to see her only child finally tie the knot. She would have been more excited to come if I was getting married because of a pregnancy. However, Marcus and I had already gotten the discussion about kids out of the way, and he was visibly relieved to find out I had no desire to be a mother. Not only that, he "jokingly" remarked, "I think if we had a kid and some serious discipline was in order, I'd be so furious I'd do something drastic,

`a la strangle him and roast him or her for dinner." He pro-
ceeded to laugh but only after I must have looked positively
horrified.

The cocktail and dinner party tonight, was being handled
by "Megan's Catering." Five purportedly "high-profile" couples had been invited, their names unrecognizable to me.
Marcus claimed he couldn't handle a cocktail and dinner
party for five couples plus us, given that the couples were
"important." Also he was "on call." Something didn't seem
right, but I could never get myself to question what my own
husband was up to! Only if I suspected he was cheating on
me, would I have pressed him for details. As it stood, I still
didn't know for sure what the hell Marcus' exact relationship
was with his rich boss who lived "up the mountain."
    I used to think any get-togethers Marcus planned, were
opportunities for him to cook "for fun," even if it was just
appetizers for the cocktail parties. I figured he had to test
new recipes on someone, so why not friends? He'd mentioned how he should publish a cookbook of his best recipes,
but he was actually "afraid" it would be a bestseller. He
didn't want anyone to know who he was. I identified with
that notion but lately wondered if I ever had any idea what
he was really thinking. Regarding this particular evening, I
was wondering more than ever. As it was, he typically
obsessed over every single detail of any party he had. To
leave everything to someone else? Unheard of.
    Fortunately the dining table was large enough to seat
everyone, and we had plenty of dinnerware, two details I had
in mind. I assumed Marcus did, too. Or maybe there was
something else going on in his head.
    All this collective stress compelled me to confront Marcus
after the party, to find out exactly what the situation was
with his boss, whether he owned this house, etc. I was
beyond sick of it! I'd dusted the artwork in the house enough

times to get a really good look at all of it and had eventually written down some "names and numbers." If everything in here was authentic, Marcus was either extremely well-off or was at one point and spent every last cent on his art collection. The third alternative was none of it was his, nor was the house. I maintained the possibility of the latter, thanks to a question I'd posed to him a few days earlier, about a simple home improvement: replacing the ivory carpet in the guest bedroom and bathroom. My mother was the only person who'd stayed with us, but the carpet had looked worn and dirty from the day I saw it. Rather than clean it, why not replace it? Those were the only two rooms that had carpet; the remainder had wood flooring or granite tile.

Medium-gray-colored carpet was what I had in mind, nothing expensive. Between that and the modest size of the two rooms, it didn't seem like it would have been a big deal. Nevertheless, Marcus hemmed and hawed when the proposition was made, so clearly it was a big deal. Either that or we were moving soon.

How could a party not be a success if "someone else" (Megan's Catering) took care of everything? It sort of was, as in all the guests appeared to enjoy themselves. Meanwhile, I liked to think I did a good job of pretending to enjoy myself right along with them. Thankfully all the tall, stick-thin wives of these supposed bigwigs, sat more than they stood, as Marcus kept the cocktail part of the party brief and made sure everyone sat down for dinner A.S.A.P. It was the first time Marcus looked anything but relaxed. No one but me appeared to discern as much, however.

Unlike one of the guests, Gart Osher, I did not get drunk. I couldn't afford to, given my resolve to confront Marcus once and for all about what the hell he did for a living (and all that it entailed).

By eleven, the caterers had packed up and left, doing an

excellent job of leaving the place spotless. The guests had departed as well, save for Gart and his wife, Kim. He was so smashed he couldn't drive them home to Carefree, about fifteen miles north. They'd arrived in a new, silver Porsche 911 Turbo with a manual transmission. Kim drank only one glass of wine, but she couldn't drive a stick-shift. Since I could, I wanted to drive the car back to their place, while Marcus drove them in his Mercedes.

Marcus made it clear with a wink and a head shake, he wanted no part of helping get the Oshers home – most likely because he was "on call." A cab had been called and should have been arriving any minute. Given the steep, dark, winding driveway, it would be difficult to locate the residence, although there were large, reflective address numbers on one of the two-foot, cream-colored, concrete-block pillars on either side of the end of the driveway. I was all for calling the cab company to make sure the driver was showing up, but Marcus pulled me into the kitchen and told me not to. He looked absolutely furious I'd even brought it up, making me more certain than ever something was going on and not just in my imagination.

Meanwhile, Kim looked tired and exasperated, but her husband appeared comparatively wide-awake as he scoured the bar in the corner of the living room, searching for one last drink. I decided to go upstairs and change into more comfortable footwear. Marcus could keep the Oshers company, although he didn't seem too concerned about as much and kept going out on the patio. I hadn't a clue what the hell he was doing, besides gazing at the stars. Obviously nothing was going to make any sense this evening.

As soon as I was upstairs, it was tempting to call it a night, change into my pajamas and hop in bed, versus just change my shoes and return to my hostess duties, downstairs. One advantage to having Megan's Catering show up, was the minimal clean-up. Seconds later there was the sound of glass breaking, downstairs.

Standing with my back to the doorway of the walk-in closet, I jumped when I felt "someone" place his hands on my waist. Marcus whispered, "I want to thank you for putting up with so many guests tonight. I know they were a lot to handle. Especially that particular group." Then he kissed the back of my head.

"Aren't you worried about the mess Gart just made?" I couldn't help asking. I was too skeptical at this point to get lost in the moment.

"I'll get to it," Marcus offered, actually sounding enthused about as much, definitely highly unusual. "The cab driver knocked right after, and he helped Kim take Gart to the car. I'm going back downstairs and lock up and get the broken glass. I'll be back as soon as I finish everything."

I nodded, resigned. There was something about not seeing my husband's face when he said what he did, that left me doubting. At this point, why not?

Nevertheless, I remained hopeful this day could be redeemed, and I changed into a favorite nightgown of Marcus'. It was above the knee, frilly, sheer black silk, etc. Even someone like me felt sexy when wearing it. At the same time it was not a first choice for comfortable sleepwear. A pair of long or short-sleeved, cotton pajamas was my favorite.

The aforementioned scratchy nightgown was exactly what I ended up wearing to bed because I fell asleep waiting for Marcus to return!

My dear husband woke me the next morning about seven A.M., saying, "Elsa, wake up. We have to go. Now. We can only take what'll fit in two or three suitcases."

Initially I was disoriented and barely paid attention to what I'd just been told. I was more concerned with the fact the plantation shutters over the window above the bed, were left open, allowing the sunlight to stream in. It only added to this unwanted news. Unfortunately, the news wasn't entirely

71

surprising. Marcus had either been fired since I last saw him or he abruptly quit. Given his strange behavior prior to this, possibly his quitting wasn't so sudden, after all.

Then Marcus turned. I'd been focusing on him as I tried to shake my grogginess, and I was fully awake when noticing there was what appeared to be dried blood all over his tan pants and white shirt, "the remainder" of what he'd worn the night before, for the party. He either slaughtered a small calf for his boss' late-night dinner, or his boss was the victim. Either option sounded horrible, but I had a distinct feeling the latter was the case. As it was, Marcus had complained about buying groceries for his boss, as he thought they should have been delivered. Marcus continued to frequent "Sammy's" and occasionally saw Verne, who nodded or waved at him. Marcus thought perhaps Verne purposely avoided him (out of fear) and considered that hilarious.

I suddenly became so nauseous I was forced to make a run for the bathroom. Marcus said, "I knew I could count on you, Elsa, no matter what. Just remember one thing, babe. I spent the night with you. Maybe you don't know precisely what time I slipped into bed, but it couldn't have been much after midnight because you went to bed shortly before that time and barely fell asleep before I woke you up and . . ."

If Marcus had given me any more instructions I missed them because I'd slammed the bathroom door to throw up in privacy. At least it had nothing to do with having a hangover. I would have preferred that to having a husband I passionately loved, who was also a murderer. Since I'd married him "for better or for worse," there was but one thing to do and that was start packing.

Meant for One Another

It wasn't as if Mickey Rycroft ever "planned" to have an affair. Was it something most men did plan? Only women did that. A woman needed a reason to stray and then either purposely got caught red-handed (and was forgiven) or wanted to prove she could find someone else and proceeded to move on (and not always with the person she was having the affair). Basically, women were the only ones who ever came out ahead in the cheating game. What Mickey wanted was to get back to where he was before: happily married to his wife and not having an affair simply because he'd happened upon a willing accomplice (and she was the instigator).

But that was why Mickey needed to abruptly terminate his ten-month affair. Having realized the error of his ways, he wanted nothing more to do with the twenty-year-old seductress known as "Silky." That really was her name, versus an alias. She was a clerk at "Muriel's Handbags and Accessories" on Quail Run Avenue in Paradise Valley, Arizona. Mickey had initially met her when he was at the store just before closing time, picking out a leather wallet for his wife of six years, Marina. She'd already told him specifically what style she wanted for her birthday and where to buy it. The choice of color was up to him. She'd promised not to return it unless he picked out one that was tangerine or fuchsia. Even purple was O.K., as long as the leather was soft.

"Muriel's" was the location of the affair. Conveniently there was a back room that resembled a small studio apartment, including a plush, roomy, brown leather sofa. Silky claimed the area was merely for taking breaks, but Mickey had to wonder if the store's owner, a prominent area socialite (whose first name was Muriel), encouraged her employees to use the space "after hours" if they liked, endorsing illicit behavior.

Earlier this afternoon, Mickey had called the shop and let Silky know he was stopping by. That meant he would be there around closing time, and they would fool around in the back. These encounters had occurred no more than once a week, sometimes "only" every other week.

The truth of the matter was, Mickey intended to tell Silky he had to end things with her. It was imperative he spring the news on her, versus warn her they needed to talk. Had he done more communicating with her at the onset, he'd know her better than he did. What worried him the most was his potential reaction to Silky, should she decide not to amicably end their affair. And "amicably" meant they would quietly go their separate ways. It had nothing to do with having sex "one last time." He had no interest in as much and already knew he'd lose his temper if she became pushy about the issue. He happened to have a mean streak, but he'd managed to get a handle on it mostly thanks to his wife. Marina always brought out the best in him, and until he came to his senses about this pointless dalliance, he'd started taking her for granted. Terminating the affair came with the expectation she never found out about it. That sounded like an awful lot to ask for, as he considered it.

When Mickey didn't have a rendezvous with Silky, he'd usually piddle around the house, waiting for Marina to return from work and start dinner. His wife cooked almost every night, aware of how much he enjoyed a home-cooked meal, even if it was hot dogs and beans.

Should he be "late for dinner," Mickey would tell Marina

he was having a couple beers with his buddies. When he finally came home she never failed to greet him with a kiss but never asked him why he didn't smell or taste like beer. As it was, he didn't drink much alcohol, so it should have been obvious if he had drunk even a little. Evidently she trusted him entirely. Knowing as much made Mickey feel even worse—were that possible. Meanwhile, at this point he was still a couple miles from the boutique, where Silky could hardly wait to close up so they could have sex on the sofa in the back room. Checking his watch, he was going to be earlier than usual. That was just as well; he wanted to deliver his news and go home. He'd previously told Marina he might be late but only intended to have one beer with his pals. He'd never felt like such a complete liar as when he'd told her that. It'd taken him ten months to figure out the obvious? Better late than never, he supposed.

Reaching his destination, Mickey was suddenly very nervous, as he was becoming more and more uncertain as to how Silky would take the news. He shouldn't have bothered to take a shower before coming here; doing so had become such a habit he didn't think twice. If Silky had an opportunity to see (and smell) him after a long day at a work site, maybe she'd more easily accept his announcement regarding ending their affair. Then again, there were unsettling moments when she seemed to think he was her soul mate and . . .

Marina never asked Mickey why he always came home from work and took a shower and changed clothes before meeting co-workers for a couple beers. He should have been happy he had even more proof she took him at his word, but he was only feeling more and more like a dolt. He'd been "dressed up" when he'd initially stopped in "Muriel's" because it had been Marina's birthday and he was taking her out afterward.

Mickey parked his newer, silver Ford pick-up on the left side of the shop. It was actually one of three businesses in

75

a rose-colored stucco, flat-roofed "strip mall." The other two businesses consisted of an insurance agency and a hair salon. Both were usually closed when he showed up, especially if he came on Monday, as he did today. Having parked in an out of the way spot, he took a few moments to try and relax. He didn't trust himself, feeling so tense. Even though it was barely five, there wasn't a single vehicle in front of the building, meaning Silky had already closed the store for the day, indicating she was "ready for him." Truthfully he didn't want to see her face. As a sideline, she had the nerve to confess to having "taken a few bucks" from the register on occasion, justifying doing so because she only made eight dollars an hour. Mickey didn't question her logic; what she did was wrong and he highly disapproved.

To top it off, Silky had made the first move, an important distinction. His undoing was taking her up on her offer to gift wrap the lavender-colored pigskin wallet he'd chosen for Marina. In turn, Mickey was invited to wait in the back and have a seat on the comfortable-looking, brown leather sofa. Before leaving the room, Silky had introduced herself (giving only her first name), brushing her bare arm on his as he sat down. (He was wearing a short-sleeved, cream-colored dress shirt.) When he took Marina out he'd planned to add a tie and suit coat. She liked to go to an upscale restaurant for special occasions, and her thirty-fifth birthday was just that. And she looked good for her age, not that she was "old."

Going someplace "nice" for dinner, never failed to turn Marina on, so Mickey looked forward to what might happen after the check was settled. He'd been horny as hell lately, and she'd been working longer hours at a plastic surgeon's busy office, so she was seemingly always tired. On the weekends, however, she sometimes managed to make time for him.

"Glad you like it," Silky said in response to Mickey's compliment of her gift-wrapping skills. She'd brought him the present while he'd patiently sat on the sofa, albeit on the edge of it. (He wasn't even aware he'd looked as if he was getting ready to make a run for it.)

As soon as Silky handed him the gift and he started to stand, she kissed him right on the lips! Not two seconds later, she literally fell on him and "forced him" to make out with her. Fortunately Marina's present wasn't fragile because it ended up inadvertently flung across the room.

Dinner with Marina was a disaster. Actually, what happened (or didn't) after they dined out was the real issue. The biggest problem was Mickey felt guilty he couldn't satisfy his wife. It was extremely embarrassing, not only thanks to his physical dilemma. He should have confessed to his wife about the affair, right then and there. A big issue was her damned present, something she'd badly wanted. Mickey had taken it to the restaurant so she could open it while having dessert. She ended up not wanting dessert, which was unusual for her on "a special occasion." So when she received her gift over a cup of decaf, there was hollowness to the presentation. Or maybe his guilt had gone into overdrive.

Marina had to endlessly reassure Mickey his lack of ability to sexually perform was "no big deal." Her reassurances had only made him feel so guilty he could hardly stand it! Again, however, he passed up the opportunity to confess to his indiscretion while it was still in the early going. That alone would have forced him to end it.

The next day, Marina got ready for work like everything was O.K. Meanwhile, Mickey happened to be "between jobs" and was off work for most of the week. He'd had plenty of time to think but rather than do any mental delving, he watched TV and took his share of long naps.

Feeling distracted all day, Marina couldn't wait to get off work, although the end was still a ways away. She'd been distracted a lot lately and chalked it up to the fact she needed a break from her job. Sometimes it was so tedious, especially when a potential patient wanted "work done" but was already perfect!

During lunch at her desk (a diet Coke, an orange, and exactly three dozen roasted almonds), Marina made the mistake of turning on her cell phone. Usually she left it off or charged it. For a change everyone else left for lunch, so she must have been feeling lonely.

None other than Janet Keel (her maiden name) called, Marina's best friend from high school. They were still quite close, although their busy lives kept them from getting together very often.

Janet became a "Shearman" when she married a highly-reputable cardiologist, fourteen years her senior, with two sons in college. He was a widower who'd lost his beloved wife Patricia to cancer when their boys were in junior high. Janet was set up with the doctor via her older brother, who was also a cardiologist. She was only supposed to go out to dinner with him so he wouldn't be so lonely. Their date had occurred shortly after the man's younger son had left home to start his first year of college. Janet's brother was well-aware his sister didn't have much interest in ever marrying, and his colleague had repeatedly maintained he was fine being an empty-nester and a widower, in rather short order.

Sparks evidently flew because the two shocked everyone by announcing in practically no time at all, they were engaged to be married. Soon afterward they were man and wife.

That was just over a year ago, and Janet should have been elated to be married to such a great guy. No one seemed to have a bad word to say about her husband, Todd, except her. Marina had even started to wonder how she could have been good friends with such a selfish bitch.

Just when Marina started to think maybe she was being too hard on Janet, none other than the selfish sow herself said, "I felt like I had to talk to *somebody* after what I just did. With how I feel, I don't know if I should be proud or ashamed."

"What happened?" Marina asked in all innocence, not paying any attention to exactly what Janet was trying to infer.

"I just had white-hot sex with the super-hot hunk of a sprinkler repairman!" Janet could hardly wait to proclaim. "My husband made the appointment, and I was expected to be home and tell the hottie what the problem was! Todd knows how I hate to have to relate a problem to any repair people, so I thought after a year of marriage, it was high time for some revenge. So I not only greeted the guy in a leopard-print bikini, I hung on his every word until I could sneak in a kiss. I was so lucky this guy was who he was. I mean, I don't show off for just anyone, despite what I just told you! Anyway, it all paid off in a very big way!"

As Janet continued to brag about her sexual exploits, Marina decided it was "high time" to charge her phone, so she hit the "end" button and plugged in the charger for the drive home.

The second half of Marina's work day moved more quickly than the first, which helped matters. Still, once five o'clock arrived, she couldn't wait to leave. She was actually looking forward to making dinner, a task she typically dreaded. Were she an excellent cook, perhaps it would have changed her outlook. Was it time for a cooking class? Marina was willing to try anything to bring Mickey and her closer again, as they'd definitely drifted apart – to the point he no longer even appeared to be attracted to her! That hurt, more than he had any idea. Even a little cuddling was out of the question, and the more she'd thought about everything (doing so had helped make the afternoon pass), his "disinterest" in her had begun shortly after her birthday, which was a good ten months ago. She never stopped to think about how much time had passed. She'd complain of a headache every so often, and Mickey was always lock-step with her, as far as not being "in the mood" for any intimacy. After hearing Janet proudly reveal her dalliance with a sprinkler repairman, it suddenly became a definite possibility Mickey was having an affair.

Finally on her way home, Marina's biggest barrier was all the traffic, but she vowed not to let it get to her. However, never before was she forced to wade through traffic jams while simultaneously compelled to ponder whether her husband was a philanderer! That notion alone upset her so much, she almost jammed her foot on the accelerator before the light at the intersection had changed—and she was fourth (at least) in line.

Then her phone rang. It was an unfamiliar local number, but she answered it anyway, only to hear: "Marina, are you at work or are you on your way home?" The desperate-sounding caller was none other than Mickey, but it took a second to recognize his voice! She couldn't help but become worried.

"I'm driving right now," Marina replied. "I left work a few minutes ago."

"I need your help," Mickey told her. "I . . . I think I accidentally killed someone."

"What?" Marina asked, not believing what she just heard. Then her phone abruptly dropped the call. Only she got to do that! It wasn't like she was in the middle of nowhere. She was so frustrated it was hard not to toss the damned phone out the window.

Finally everyone started moving again. Since she was in the right lane, the logical thing to do was turn into the first driveway, which was for a cluster of one-story, tan stucco office buildings and an adjacent parking lot. There she could collect herself. If Mickey didn't call her back in a few seconds, she'd call him at the number that had come up on the phone screen.

That was unnecessary, as he called back the moment she

pulled into the parking lot. The first thing he said was, "I know this is a lot for you to take, but could you listen for a minute and not hang up on me?"

"I am! I was! The signal got lost," Marina replied, incensed it even occurred to her husband she would "hang up on him" at what was obviously a critical time.

"It's a long story," Mickey went on to say, as if oblivious to what he was just told. "Please come here and help me."

"Where the hell are you?"

"I hate to have to tell you, but it's part of 'the long story.'"

So Marina found herself continuing westbound on Lincoln Road, headed for "Muriel's Handbags and Accessories," just off Lincoln, on Quail Run Avenue. She loved to browse but rarely bought anything. That was why she'd put in a request for a new wallet from there for her birthday, which was several months ago. Now she had to go there to help her husband because he might have killed someone? She liked the abstract idea of him having an affair, better. The more she thought about everything, there was a distinct possibility those separate circumstances went together.

Given some extra time to think, Marina put more and more "clues" together regarding Mickey's behavior and wondered why it didn't occur to her a long time ago, he might have been cheating on her. Thanks was owed to Janet for this epiphany; apparently it didn't take much for someone to abandon his or her moral standard.

Truth be told, Marina was in shock. Mickey always seemed to live for his job and making good money, not caring about much else besides the fact everything they owned was paid for. On occasion he liked to go out for a couple beers with some co-workers but rather than just show up dirty and sweaty from doing construction work all day, he'd stop home first and take a shower. She used to think that was considerate of him since it wasn't like he was otherwise fastidious. However, it was interesting he never smelled like he'd been in a bar when he'd return home. She always figured that was because he'd taken a shower right before leaving.

Traffic had continued to be congested until Marina missed a light at the intersection of Lincoln and Hummingbird, making her first in line. As soon as the light changed, she couldn't help but take advantage of the relatively open road by accelerating more and more, not paying any attention to how fast she was going. Driving a newer, white Honda Civic, she hardly stood out, given the make and model of the car and the fact there were a lot of white vehicles in the Phoenix valley.

Glancing in her rearview mirror, Marina happened to notice flashing lights. At first she thought it was for an ambulance but soon realized there was a squad car right behind her Civic. It just so happened this part of Lincoln Road was flat and the few options for places to turn, mostly consisted of driveways leading to private residences. Marina was aware she was supposed to stop for the police, but she was compelled to find a place to turn off the four-lane road.

After a hundred yards she gave up and flipped on her right-turn signal and stopped. The whole situation had her so stressed she felt faint. It was imperative she get her act together before the officer approached her window.

"License and registration?" Marina was asked by the cop, looking down at her from outside her car. She wished her Honda were a Maserati, if only right at this moment, to help make her humiliation more bearable.

Handing the officer the requested identification, she watched him take it and look it over before asking her, "Do you know why I pulled you over?"

"I never speed, but I admit I am in kind of a hurry, so I was probably going too fast," Marina replied, praying absolute honesty would save her ass.

"Is there a reason you're in such a hurry you were going

more than twenty over the speed limit?"

"Was I?" Marina asked, surprised she was moving that fast. She wasn't trying to be a smart-aleck; she honestly didn't think she'd been going at quite such a clip. Then she told him, "I just got a call from my husband . . . from his job. He wasn't specific, but he urged me to come immediately. He stopped just short of telling me it's an emergency."

The police officer appeared to buy right into what she'd told him, as he said, "I'm going to do some checking and I'll be right back."

While Marina waited for the officer to return, she couldn't help continually looking in the left rearview mirror, hoping she'd see him approach. She didn't even care if she ended up with a ticket; she just wanted to be on her way.

Finally he returned. Handing over Marina's paperwork the cop said, "You had nothing on your record, so I'm going to take you at your word, your husband needs your help. Nevertheless, slow down and be safe."

"Thank you, I will," Marina told the officer. She was much more grateful and relieved than she sounded. All she had to do was reach "Muriel's Handbags and Accessories" without any more mishaps, and it was only about another mile away.

Mickey was standing in the doorway of "Muriel's" when Marina arrived. Her heart leaped, realizing her husband was not kidding around about having "accidentally killed someone." She couldn't imagine what circumstances led to this. Noticing his truck parked on the left side of the building, Marina wondered if none other than Muriel was "the other woman," and Mickey met her here. If that was the case, her death would be front-page news, no matter how much anyone tried to downplay it. She was a wealthy socialite, married to a very successful Phoenix businessman. Owning her shop was "a hobby."

As Marina neared the entryway of the store, Mickey said, "The alarm was on, but I was able to de-activate it, thanks to coincidentally watching Silky set the code a few times."

"Silky's her name?" Marina asked, unable to help sounding a bit shrill.

"Yeah," Mickey replied.

It was more than apparent he was only worried about hustling Marina into the store and locking the door; if he really did kill someone, did he actually expect to get by with it? Unlike her, he'd let his passport expire. He should have considered renewing it before knocking someone off, even if it was "unintentional." The border of Mexico was too close not to take advantage of, should the need arise.

As Mickey indicated for her to follow him to the back of the store, Marina asked him, "Why don't we just call the police? If it was an accident and you can explain yourself, you'll be better off, versus trying to pretend nothing ever happened."

"I don't want to do any pretending," Mickey told her. "I want to somehow eliminate the evidence. That's why I called you. I was hoping you could help me brainstorm."

Marina could only shake her head. What happened to the relatively practical-minded man she'd married? Murdering Silky must have done this to him. Most likely he was in shock. Nonetheless, Marina was having a hard time feeling sorry for either one of these individuals. Maybe she was the sick one.

It turned out Mickey led Marina to "the back room" of the store, which resembled a den. There was a brown leather sofa; a brass floor lamp; an oak end table on either side of the sofa; and a large, tan, faux-fur throw rug in front of the sofa. In the far corner to the left of the rear exit there was a small kitchen area. Obviously this was more than just a break room.

She was so busy looking around, initially Marina didn't even notice the lifeless female body lying face-down on the rug. The woman's shoulder-length, brunette hair was loose, and something about it covering her face, really freaked out

Marina. And all this was assuming her husband's girlfriend was indeed dead. It was hard to believe Mickey could be so shallow as to even have an affair. She liked to think she'd married a better man than that.

This "girl" on the floor obviously was in no better shape than Marina. If anything, Marina was slimmer, a couple inches taller and had longer legs. Never in a million years would Marina have worn a pair of low-rise jeans as body-hugging as Silky's. Silky also wore a short-sleeved, loose-fitting, navy blue top, compelling Marina to wonder if this chick was wearing "maternity wear" (despite the tight jeans). No, that wasn't possible. Mickey absolutely didn't want to ever be a dad just like Marina never wanted to be a mom. At the same time, how the hell could anyone have predicted what this Silky broad wanted? It was possible she'd tricked Mickey by getting pregnant and proceeded to confront him. Of course he couldn't accept the news, given his type-A personality. Shortsighted Silky didn't know that because she'd only concerned herself with getting laid.

"What happened?" Marina finally asked. Otherwise it appeared they would be standing before Silky's lifeless body, indefinitely.

"It's a long story," Mickey replied.

"I know!" Marina said, not hiding her impatience. It was bad enough Mickey had been screwing the woman lying here supposedly dead, yet he continued tiptoeing around the issue? Something had evidently made him snap, and Marina was positively furious with him. Obviously he couldn't control himself, despite the fact he'd mellowed.

Meanwhile, Mickey looked completely undone by the tone of Marina's response. Still, he had no idea the extent of her fury. It was humiliating not to have a clue your husband was cheating. Marina couldn't believe she never suspected anything.

She couldn't resist asking, "Are you sure she's dead?"

"Of course!" Mickey told her.

"Did you strangle her?"

"Why would you need to know that?"

"I'm just trying to figure out how many prints you have on her," Marina told him.

"Didn't I already tell you I want to 'eliminate the evidence'?" Mickey retorted, not hiding his irritation. "I wanted you to come here so we could decide together where the best place would be to take her body and make it disappear. I can't help remarking it appears you have some familiarity with all this."

"I watch more crime shows than you, is all," Marina told him. "It's not like I'm running around looking for trouble, like you appear to be doing . . . How about The Grand Canyon for losing her body?"

"That's a great idea!" Mickey exclaimed. "We could leave now, get a room about halfway there and be up early to drive the rest of the way."

"I wasn't going to say it aloud, but since you just went this far, have you lost your mind?" Marina implored. "I wasn't going to outright ask you that, but I can't stand it anymore. I don't feel like I'm talking to Mickey. I feel like I'm . . ."

The phone rang in the other room. Mickey turned as if to head in that direction, only to abruptly halt when Marina asked him, "Where the hell are you going? Isn't the store 'closed' for the day?"

Nodding, Mickey told her, "Yeah, it is. I just wanted to answer it in case someone otherwise decides to stop by here looking for Silky."

"So you answer the phone? Then your alibi's shot to hell."

"Yeah, you're right," Mickey admitted. "See? I knew I needed you here to help me. Marina, I promise I'll make all this up to you and hopefully you'll forgive me."

After the phone rang a couple more times and finally stopped, Marina told her cheating husband, "I hope you know you have your work cut out for you."

"I don't blame you," he said. "Just thinking of a story for why Silky might disappear but leave her car parked behind 'Muriel's' seems to be taking more brain cells than I have."

"Who even knows you've been meeting her here?" Marina asked. "I sure as hell didn't know, but looking back, I should have at least been suspicious of something."

"I'm *sorry*, O.K.?" Mickey told her. "It was the kind of situation that just sort of started and then repeating it was too easy."

"So you had to kill her?"

"Come on, Marina," Mickey said, sounding like she'd said something out of line. Given the fact he'd killed someone (by strangulation most likely because there was no bloody mess and he didn't own a gun—unlike herself), Marina didn't feel as if any question she asked was "off limits." And since they were "husband and wife," she'd assumed they "had to" openly communicate. What a joke.

Nevertheless, it wasn't too late to attempt to make amends. It would undoubtedly be a requirement of any marriage counselor, having them discuss their respective shortcomings. Mickey would have preferred being dragged to Hell than attend counseling with her, so she'd have to take matters into her own hands.

"How did things get to this point?" Marina asked, as she sat on the sofa. (It was very comfortable.) "I think you owe me some sort of 'explanation' before anything else."

With Mickey apparently confused by what was said, Marina added, "I sorta have a timeline in my head, as to when all this started, but I need to know what events led to this. And if you wanted to end this affair, why didn't you just tell her over the phone, to avoid the obvious temptation to choke her to death?"

"I didn't! I . . ."

"Why hide how you killed her?" Marina wanted to know.

"What is this obsession of yours with strangulation?"

Mickey asked.

"You know I hate when you do that."

"What?"

"Are you trying to dig yourself an even deeper hole?"

"I . . ."

"Don't even bother to ask me another question," Marina told her husband. "You know I don't like when you ask me a question after *I* ask a question. Since you made me come here, it's time you have a seat and tell me everything."

"*Everything*?" Mickey asked, looking more anxious than ever.

"Mostly just the events leading up to *strangling* this poor woman," Marina replied. "I just want to try to understand how it could all come to this."

Finally Mickey sat down beside his wife and attempted to quell his anxiety long enough to tell her what had happened: "I'd finally seen the error of my ways, and I'd met Silky here today to tell her we had to end things. I knew she'd never end it over the phone, and the only way she wouldn't suspect something was if I acted like I was meeting her for sex. The problem started after I told her we couldn't see each other anymore, and I refused her offer to have sex one last time. I got so mad at her for making a big deal out of me attempting to right a wrong, I choked her. I never intended to kill her . . . I was just trying to temporarily shut her up." Afterward, he leaned over and put his face in his hands.

Rather than put an arm around Mickey or console him in some other manner, Marina stood and asked him, "Am I correct in concluding you started this affair about ten months ago?"

"Yes. I'd come here for your birthday present," Mickey replied, sounding as if he deserved to be less guilty because of as much. Then he added, "She seduced me! I know that's no excuse . . . I felt so bad afterward . . ."

"You couldn't have sex with me, right?" Marina asked, annoyed.

Her emotions were lost on Mickey, who readily replied, "Yes! That's right!"

"Am I expected to assume you're really repenting?" Marina asked. "If your heart is in the right place, why not call nine-one-one and explain what happened?"

"I can't imagine anyone believing me, as far as making a mistake and accidentally killing Silky," Mickey said. "Just explaining myself would sound so horrible."

"You're innocent until proven guilty," Marina reminded him, although reassuring her wayward husband was the last thing on her mind. She was occupied with doing something else.

Marina never could have anticipated her marriage would end like it just did. Although she'd predicted Mickey would die before her, she never in a million years would have guessed it'd happen at her hand.

One bullet to the side of Mickey's head took him out. He proceeded to fall on the sofa, his head conveniently landing on the armrest opposite to where Marina had been sitting. She wasn't positive he was actually dead, but she was reluctant to shoot him a second time. So far there was hardly any blood, and she preferred it that way. The last thing she wanted to do was make a mess. She'd check his pulse in a minute. Unlike her husband, she'd make good on as much and knew what she was doing. (She'd attended college to be a nurse but never got her degree.)

Right after Marina put the revolver back in her purse, Silky began to stir. Marina was too overcome by everything to be surprised. If anything she was initially relieved. Then it occurred to her she just unnecessarily killed her husband. She should have checked Silky's pulse before letting emotions override reason.

Before Silky sat up, Marina was out of here. Those two had deserved one another all along.

89

Amy Kristoff

The Ultimate Diet Pill

"I need a very small-adult casket," Andrew Cassel told the undertaker, Morton Cower, of Golden Sunset Funeral Home/Cemetery/Crematory in Scottsdale, Arizona. It was conveniently located by the 101 Freeway. In fact, an exit ramp circled right over a portion of it, creating a unique juxtaposition. Only in a desert environment could such a sight have appeared normal.

Andrew was invited to follow Mr. Cower to "the casket showroom," of which the latter was extremely proud. Looking around, Andrew said, "None of these will be small enough."

"This is for your wife, you mentioned over the phone?"

"Right," Andrew replied. "But she wasn't a midget or little person or whatever the hell the politically-correct term is nowadays. She literally shrunk in size, shape and everything else, all thanks to some stupid purple diet pill she took to be thin and young-looking again."

Sensing Mr. Cassel's distress, Morton, ever the sympathizer, was quick to offer his reassurances: "I'm only trying to confirm your needs, Mr. Cassel. Often times, folks are reluctant to reveal they need a casket for let's say a child, because they feel like it's their fault the child died, no matter the circumstances. So what I'm saying is if you would just bear with me and let me help you, I will make absolutely certain this experience will be as pleasant as possible, considering the emotionally devastating circumstances."

Fine. Andrew was ready to do business with this guy.

Losing his wife like Andrew did, made the whole situation hard to accept. It was as if there was a second reality occurring alongside "the real one." As it was, having lost his soul mate, Andrew no longer felt like there was a reality. All he could do was get used to this new one.

After some discussion, it was decided the best way to preserve Shirley Cassel's integrity was to have a closed casket. It was that or else cremation, which Andrew couldn't have agreed to under any circumstances. Since Shirley didn't have a will, she'd never specified wanting to be cremated, anyway.

Morton Cower knew best. It was how he made a living (no pun intended). If Andrew Cassel was uncomfortable having his wife's body cremated, so be it. Personally, Morton considered cremation the most respectful way to say goodbye to a loved one who had passed under extraordinary circumstances. However, he'd go out of business if he let his opinions get in the way. As it was, how could anyone preserve the dignity of a woman who was once 5'4" but whose body shrunk to a mere 5 ¼", her proportions equally diminished? Astounding.

Even though Andrew wanted to avoid putting Shirley's tiny body through an autopsy, it was made "a requirement" by one authority or another. All he knew was he never should have joked about her pudgy figure, as she obviously took it way too much to heart. And he'd gained weight right along with her, as they both liked to eat out far more than they liked to exercise. "A miracle diet pill," however, was a seemingly easy, quick answer to weight-loss. The small, purple-colored pills didn't turn out to be anything but a nightmare for Shirley. That said, the nightmare really started after she'd lost the first twenty pounds. (Her goal had been to lose forty.) Since those twenty came off so easily, it encouraged her to go ahead with her goal. Meanwhile, after Andrew lost his initial twenty pounds (his goal was to lose fifty), he was so undone by how effortlessly the weight came off, he stopped taking the pills. The weird part was he'd barely eaten any less and hadn't even started exercising. Off the pills, he vowed to begin (and keep) an exercise regimen as well as keep a better eye on his calorie intake.

As for Shirley, she started taking the diet pills at the same time Andrew did, having received a "two-for-one order" in the mail. She'd called the toll-free number for the diet pill manufacturer within ten minutes of hearing an ad for the pills on the radio. Andrew was in fact with her, as they were returning from a Friday morning shopping trip to a major discount retailer. It was something that had become a weekly ritual, ever since he agreed to cut his hours at the accounting firm. He wanted to retire at sixty, so Shirley and he could do some traveling. In the meantime Andrew was more than happy to let the young associates pick up the slack.

Andrew didn't have the energy to become vindictive and sue the diet pill manufacturer, even though several friends told him he needed "to get a good lawyer and go after the company." Meanwhile, he did some research online and couldn't find a single complaint about "The Magic Purple Diet Pill," made by "Ultimate Diet Company." Nonetheless, he felt like he lost his wife twice: first by her dying; second, how she went, given the seemingly impossible circumstances.

Not to make excuses for something he did, but Andrew sort of aided Shirley in her demise, once he was aware there was no reversing the unwelcome side-effects of the diet pill. Shirley became so physically diminished (shrunken to a miniature version of herself), it was difficult to see her. She'd been examined by several physicians and it had been agreed, there was nothing that could be done to reverse the effects of the drug. Her body, having reacted like it did, only had like one in a billion chances of doing so. It was a shame those odds worked in her favor in this case versus winning the lottery—not that money mattered if you didn't have your health.

In Shirley's defense, she tried to remain upbeat but felt weak and tired, leaving her miserable. No longer could she go out in public nor could she drive. It was necessary she hand-sew outfits, using scraps of material (even a yard of material was more than she needed). Shirley liked to sew but only using her machine. Thanks to how tiny she was, it was no longer safe for her to be near her sewing machine, not that she could have used it.

Andrew could have gone on and on, relating stories of how Shirley's life had changed since she'd shrunk to five and a quarter inches. It was absolutely heartbreaking for both of them. Also, she kept having severe heart palpitations, which the doctors agreed would lead to fatal cardiac arrest if she wasn't admitted to the hospital. However, she refused to go because she didn't want to lie in a humongous bed in a cold, indifferent environment, "waiting for the end."

It was hard for Andrew to even look at his tiny wife and not start crying like a baby. He loved her so much, yet he couldn't stop feeling as if he had a hand in this nightmare, thanks to his big mouth. Let her be her pudgy self. It wasn't as if he didn't love her no matter what. He was determined his off-handed remarks were what compelled her to diet, more than anything else.

Finishing up the shrub-clipping task for the oleander bushes on the far side of the driveway, Andrew had Shirley's "help." She'd been lying down most of the morning, following a sleepless night, due to constant heart palpitations and chest pain. Andrew had repeatedly offered to take her to the hospital or call an ambulance, but she was staying put. He felt the best thing he could do at this point was heed her wishes. The doctors had privately met with Andrew and warned him it was doubtful she'd live more than a month or six weeks in her condition, whether or not she was admitted to the hospital.

Not to criticize a person in this predicament, but Shirley

had basically become a nag, thanks to her diminished size and proportions. At times it was difficult to tolerate her, but Andrew tried not to let it show. It wasn't as if he didn't feel extremely sorry about what had happened to her. At the same time, she shouldn't have been so greedy about losing more and more weight. Through it all, she didn't lose her deep voice, which could become quite loud when she was angry and desperate (almost all the time, in her diminished state). A heavy smoker for twenty years, she'd quit the habit cold turkey one day, for no better reason than she was tired of lighting up (and doing so was a waste of money). Thankfully Andrew never picked up the smoking habit. His biggest vice was a propensity to overeat, especially if he didn't have enough to do.

So many conflicting thoughts were going through Andrew's head as he was completing the yard work, it wasn't too surprising he proceeded to take a step backward and practically lose his balance, yet he was first and foremost worried about not stepping on Shirley. He was that preoccupied, although he was constantly aware of his wife's general location. She'd been picking up a clipping here and there, gathering them into a pile. She was barely contributing to completing the task, but at least she was getting some fresh air and they were spending time together.

It was thanks to his damned rubber slip-on shoes, Andrew lost his balance yet again and finally fell backward. As it was, he wasn't into yard work but the current landscape company only mowed and trimmed, leaving the remainder of the yard maintenance. Given how cheap Andrew could be, the savings were worth the trade-off. Besides, there was more house than there was yard, which was fine because Andrew and Shirley didn't have a dog or any other pets. And they had no desire to spend much time outside as it was.

Just as Andrew was about to land on his butt, he managed to regain his balance – but not before really pushing on his left heel, right on the concrete driveway. Unfortunately there was something rather squishy underneath, and he was pretty sure he heard a muffled-sounding yelp.

Once he finally got his bearings, Andrew turned around to find Shirley lying on the driveway, having extreme difficulty breathing while her body wildly convulsed. Even though Andrew had taken a class in CPR, how the hell was he supposed to administer mouth-to-mouth to someone who was the size of a small doll? Besides, would it do any good? So he ran in the house and dialed 9-1-1. As much as Shirley had attempted to avoid going to the hospital, finally there was no avoiding it.

Losing his Shirley had a profound effect on Andrew. The least he could do was splurge on a casket, even though it would be closed for the wake. He chose a gorgeous (but pricey), rose-colored one. It was undeniably much more expensive than what he'd had in mind, but what the hell. Thinking like this was unprecedented.

Deciding on a casket was the most important part of the burial arrangement, as far as Andrew was concerned. Then he realized neither Shirley nor he had a burial plot. Their parents on both sides of their families had never purchased any extra plots where they were buried, in two separate cemeteries. He didn't care for either cemetery and was fine with purchasing two plots here at Golden Sunset. Shirley would have been O.K. with this place, too. She never was hard to please and would have agreed to a plot "under a viaduct," which was the location of some plots, as the cemetery was here before the 101 Freeway was constructed.

Andrew went ahead and wrote a check "for everything" and it wasn't an insignificant amount. Nonetheless he felt pretty good, considering the fact he lost the most important person in his life, under very extraordinary circumstances. His positive mood continued on the drive home. Somehow, he started thinking about Shirley's older sister, Michelle, who lived in San Francisco. She was the first person he'd called after Shirley passed away. However, Michelle had no idea her sister was overwhelmed by physical problems prior to her demise. All Michelle knew was her sister had been taking "a special diet pill," which had affected Shirley's heart because she'd had a previously undetected heart condition. Michelle was incredulous about as much, which wasn't surprising because Andrew made it up! Still, he managed to get her to agree it was indeed possible, however remotely. He highly doubted she'd demand to see the autopsy results. If she wanted to know why the casket was closed, he'd have to spontaneously think of something.

In fact, Andrew needed to call Michelle when he got home and let her know Shirley's final burial arrangements had been made. Michelle had requested an ongoing update on the latest happenings so she could make the necessary travel arrangements. Even though she freely admitted to having a fear of flying, she would have to do so in order to attend her sister's wake and funeral. Immediately afterward she had to return home, to prepare for a showing of her latest paintings and sculptures. She was becoming well-known in San Francisco and the surrounding area, thanks to her artistic talents. Shirley always scoffed at her sister's potential to make something of herself as an artist, but Andrew had greatly admired his sister-in-law's dedication.

When Michelle Kaylor appeared at Golden Sunset Funeral Home for her sister's wake and funeral, she appeared to waltz into the viewing room. Of course that was how Andrew saw it, as he was instantaneously attracted to her. Ridiculous! He was supposed to be grieving. It wasn't as if he ever had a roving eye when Shirley was alive. So did all hell suddenly break loose for his libido? Probably his grief was misplaced, was all. In other words, he was ogling his sister-in-law because he missed his wife so much. His attraction would soon pass. Thankfully she would be leaving after her brief visit.

Still, Michelle really looked good. Andrew couldn't help silently declaring as much while observing her from a distance. He remained at the back of the room, as he'd had to use the restroom and returned right after Michelle made her grand entrance. She looked so different from what he remembered, having seen her only a handful of times over the years. She was built like a gazelle. He always thought she wasn't much taller than Shirley, who was a chubby five-four (until the diet pills took over in the worst way). It was impossible Michelle was wearing high heels, walking like she was. She should have wobbled at least once or twice. Given his vantage point, Andrew couldn't see her feet anyway, and she was wearing super-long, sheer, black silk pants. The blouse matched her pants, and the pearl buttons matched her earrings. Somehow Andrew managed to notice all this before she'd turned and was ahead of him. He wished he'd never seen her at all, which was absurd.

A couple months after Shirley passed away, Andrew still felt as if she had gone somewhere and he missed her. However, it wasn't as if he was in denial about her death. It was a matter of letting time pass, so he could get used to the idea of losing the only person he'd ever loved.

Meanwhile, Andrew had been "kind of keeping track of" Michelle's art gallery showings and her online postings, as she had her own website. He couldn't seem to get enough of her. Things were to the point (he believed) it was necessary "to surprise her" at the next gallery showing of some of her watercolor paintings. He would have to fly to San Francisco to do so and was looking forward to as much. All that traveling he'd wanted to do once he'd retired? Finally he could make good on some of that. As it was, he'd taken an extra-early retirement because of Shirley's passing.

The seven years of blissful marriage to Michelle Kaylor (now Cassel) had no reason to end, as far as Andrew was concerned. In other words, they were perfect for one another, considering he thought it was only possible to feel that way with Shirley. Obviously there was an entirely different dynamic with high-energy Michelle, who was very independent-minded and liked her space, which was fine with Andrew at this point in his life. Thanks to her, he'd become much more health-conscious, but in the past year he'd let himself go. Dining out was still his favorite pastime, so Michelle humored him by going along. She wasn't particularly interested in food and happened to hate cooking, so it was her personal trade-off. That didn't bother Andrew because he had pursued her, giving him no reason to grumble.

Michelle's preferred form of exercise was to use a treadmill, which Andrew had purchased for her as a Christmas gift, the first year they were married. He'd done so to dispense of her need to go to a gym, where she formerly exercised. He just wanted to please her. As it was, she was forced to uproot herself from San Francisco and move to Andrew's Phoenix home. It was in an enclave known as Arcadia, with its citrus groves, spacious yards, and irrigation systems for maintaining all the orange and grapefruit trees. There were also plenty of sidewalks and bicycle lanes, inducing residents to get outside and exercise, even in the hot summer months. All in all, it was like a verdant oasis in the desert.

Andrew used to like occasionally taking walks around the neighborhood, no matter the weather, but ever since his weight began to steadily climb, he became a recluse. As for Michelle, he never could understand why she didn't want to exercise outside more than she did. Occasionally she'd take a walk or jog a couple miles but overall, she was a slave to the boring treadmill. It was the last thing he would have expected from "a true artist"—and that she definitely was. Her monetary success was second to how devoted she was to her work. Granted, she'd had some financial stability all along, but it'd had no effect on her ongoing passion for her work. Andrew loved her for that alone.

Michelle and Andrew had ended up driving to Las Vegas from Phoenix to get married. Both were embarrassed to admit, neither one had ever visited the city. They went there to get away from home but wouldn't have to make a lot of pre-arrangements. Andrew finally had an entirely enjoyable trip to take, with someone he cared about.

Over the years, Andrew remained incredulous he, of all the members of the male species, could manage to marry a gorgeous woman who had relegated herself to remaining single her whole life until he came along? That didn't even sound right. He was the first to admit to not exactly being a hunk and wasn't too affectionate, but he was honest, reliable and easygoing.

The most remarkable part was Andrew and Michelle had nothing in common. He didn't even have a whole lot in common with Shirley, but they'd had "a like mindset." Shirley was so much more laid-back than Michelle! It was amazing they were even sisters but they were – not even half-sisters. Shirley was the short, blond-haired, good-natured one; Michelle was the long-legged, mousy brown-haired, restless one. And that was the extent of her mousiness, despite Andrew's most initial impression of her.

Back to Andrew's weight problem. He needed to admit that fact or he'd only become more and more reclusive. If he failed to meet the dilemma head on, Michelle would finally be compelled to make a comment about how fat he was. As intense as she was, unlike her low-key sister, they were both extremely polite. However, Michelle had occasionally good-naturedly reminded Andrew about watching his weight. Unfortunately he'd paid no attention to her gentle reminders.

The big problem was Andrew had received last-minute news, to prepare himself (mentally) for a plane trip to New York City, where several of her watercolor paintings and some sculptures would be featured at a newly-opened gallery in Manhattan. A friend of a friend of a friend was doing a huge favor, something like that. He needed to accompany her because she had been told there would be some "name people" at the opening, and she would look "more complete" if she had her significant other with her.

Michelle had liked the sound of that suggestion, as she freely admitted to being "nervous as hell" about the most important showing thus far in her career. Andrew was initially thrilled to be of some use to his wife, as he'd felt like a slug ever since they married. That was not to say he mooched off her. Andrew lived off his retirement and took care of most of the household expenses, utilities, property taxes, etc. Michelle covered her personal expenses and bought most of the groceries. Most importantly, she provided him with some much-needed companionship. At the same time, it wasn't as if this marriage was some sort of "arrangement." Despite his comparatively frumpy appearance, they were lovers.

The bottom line: it was crunch time – or treadmill time —as Andrew absolutely had to lose some weight in the next week but refused to go outside to exercise. Also, he needed a quick-fix, such as those magical purple diet pills. In spite of what they did to Shirley, it was impossible the same thing could ever happen to him. If only he had some of those, he'd make sure to heed the warnings. Shirley supposedly did, but she got impatient and greedy, which was her downfall. He vowed to be patient but admittedly didn't have the luxury of much time, as he'd mentioned. It was real simple: he shouldn't have let himself go. Given Michelle's ambition, something like this was bound to happen eventually, as in he would be expected to present himself with her. He was so proud of her and wanted her to be proud of him in New York.

Half-heartedly Andrew put on a pair of black cotton jogging pants and a matching black hoodie, having changed from his white silk pajamas. He often wore pajamas until it was time to get ready to go out to dinner. Although he had a pair of "walking shoes" somewhere, he preferred to use the stupid treadmill wearing his white cotton socks. Or was that "a safety hazard"? Oh please! He found the treadmill so detestable, it had been difficult to buy it for Michelle, even though it was the only item on her Christmas list that year.

Rather than hop on the treadmill and start burning calories "the natural way," Andrew first went in search of some leftover magical purple diet pills, just in case he hid a bottle. Fortunately he never was one to throw anything away that he paid a lot of money for. And the damned purple pills weren't cheap. Thankfully Michelle hated to cook and therefore didn't dig through the kitchen shelves, looking for ingredients or utensils. After some searching, he was in fact able to find an unopened bottle of "The Magic Purple Diet Pill," still inside its cardboard container, in a back recess of the kitchen pantry. He ripped open the box, to find the expiration date on the white plastic bottle was almost five years ago. Did that mean the pills had to be disposed of, versus maybe using them this one time? He could take a couple and then see if he felt O.K.

Instead of refreshing his memory regarding the diet pill directions and warnings, Andrew tore off the plastic seal on the cap and immediately popped four pills in his mouth before grabbing a diet soda from the refrigerator. From what he remembered, you were supposed to drink water with the pills and not take them on an empty stomach. Hopefully the fact he was drinking a diet soda would offset the fact he refused to eat anything until dinner. He was too fat! And Michelle would probably agree to go out tonight. If not it would be carry-out. Either way, it was time to exercise, big-time.

The phone rang, on the kitchen wall. There was no caller I.D. in the vicinity, so he had no idea who it was. Michelle was getting more and more unsolicited calls, thanks to her growing popularity in the art world, so it was preferable to screen calls. However, he decided to answer this one.

It was Michelle! If Andrew remembered correctly, she'd gone out to buy some clothes for the trip to New York, as well as go to the hair salon. She happened to call to apprise him she was currently having her hair colored and immediately afterward would be coming home.

Andrew told his wife he loved her (which she said in return) and couldn't wait to see her.

"So what are you doing while you're waiting for me?" Michelle playfully asked, although at the same time appeared curious as to what her husband might be up to. Lately she was in fact concerned about Andrew, as he seemed depressed. She thought maybe it had something to do with him gaining some extra weight, but it was possible he was "going through one of his phases." He'd done that ever since losing his first wife, Shirley, who happened to be Michelle's sister. Shirley was the love of his life, so who could blame him?

Typically Andrew didn't hear from Michelle when she was out running errands, so her phone call was definitely unexpected. Then again, she was pretty intuitive, although she tried not to let on about it. Was there a possibility she suspected he was up to something and would suddenly rush home? Shit! Where the hell was the hair salon she liked to go to? Her stylist's name was Kiera, was all he knew.

Andrew finally answered Michelle's question by telling her the truth: "I'm scrambling to lose some weight before we go to New York City."

"So are you on the treadmill, using a cordless phone?" Michelle wanted to know. "I'd have to see that to believe it, knowing how you hate that thing . . . and phones for that matter."

"You're right, honey, I've only ever liked numbers," Andrew told his wife after swallowing four more diet pills, washed down with another diet soda. Then he said he had to go and quickly told her good-bye.

Michelle told her husband good-bye too, but he'd already hung up. Meanwhile she was getting a really bad feeling. Nonetheless, she sat through the remainder of her hair appointment, reassuring herself it wouldn't take much longer.

Once she was finally on her way, Michelle drove home like a maniac. Her aggressiveness amazed herself. If a cop pulled her over for speeding, it'd be a first, but she would have been glad to explain why she was in a big hurry. As it was, she'd recently purchased a new, silver, Audi A6, having driven used SUVs her entire adulthood. At least she finally treated herself to something worth speeding with.

Having made it home without being stopped, Michelle parked her car next to Andrew's white Ford Explorer in the garage and went in the house. The first thing she noticed while standing in the kitchen: it was way too quiet! If Andrew really was using the treadmill, he'd simultaneously be watching TV, as there was one in front of it. Michelle couldn't have exercised on the treadmill, otherwise. It was one of the few times she could watch anything. At the same time, it wasn't like she didn't enjoy exercising outside, but the older she got, she preferred to keep her exercising "private." She assumed Andrew answered her request for a treadmill because he feared she'd otherwise show off too much, either exercising outside or going to a gym. At this point she was too old to attract much attention, but there was a time when she'd go to the gym, hoping to be noticed by a potential date. But the old cliché happened to her: just when she stopped looking for love she found it. Truthfully, Michelle had been slightly in doubt she was in love with Andrew.

"Andrew? Are you home?" Michelle asked, still standing in the kitchen. The house remained quiet, so hopefully he took a walk around the block, having decided he hated the treadmill too much to use it. Or maybe he decided to scrap the idea of exercising and hopped in the shower, to get ready early to go out to dinner.

Not hearing a reply, Michelle nervously walked down the hallway from the kitchen, on her way to the exercise room. Even though this house had only one story and no basement, it was almost four-thousand square feet, which was a lot for two people. The point being "the walk" to her destination seemed like a mile.

The door to the exercise room was ajar, so Michelle pushed it open and the first thing she noticed was Andrew's black jogging suit, in the middle of the treadmill. The jogging suit was none other than a gift from her, just last Christmas. She'd given it to him as a gentle nudge to get him to exercise again.

It was just like Andrew to leave his clothes lying around. He must have started sweating and decided to take a shower, rather than bother to continue exercising.

Smiling, Michelle bent over to pick up her husband's discarded exercise clothes. Lately she'd been questioning "just how much she loved him" only because she was such an all-or-nothing kind of person (one reason she'd hesitated to ever marry). But she did indeed love him and needed him. This temporary uncertainty about his welfare, confirmed as much.

Just as Michelle grabbed the clothes, intending to ball them up and throw them in the washing machine, she could have sworn something inside them moved. Rather than investigate what it might be, she quickly flung the heap to the floor, using as much force as possible.

The Tarantula-Mouse

A glow-in-the-dark, clear acrylic computer mouse with a real tarantula inside, was a definite must-have for anyone determined to get over a fear of spiders – on his own terms. That was Nick's take on the matter, especially since he not only had that fear but spent a lot of time on computers, whether for his job or "for fun." His interests were few, but he was never bored.

Nick was about to order this very computer mouse where else but online. However, he'd initially seen it in a mail order catalog that was in the mailbox when he got home from work this evening. It was actually addressed to his uncle Ted Farris, his mother's younger brother ("or current resident"). Nick had the good fortune to inherit this two-story, three-bedroom condominium from none other than Uncle Ted. Nick had wanted to move for awhile, but he'd been waiting until he could afford it. Despite how long he'd been employed at "AZBIZ Technology," he was only now being considered for a promotion. Nick wasn't complaining; he was grateful he was able to move into a nicer place without being at the mercy of his boss.

As for the many mail order catalogs that arrived at this address all year, especially when the Christmas holiday was drawing near, Nick found it interesting his introverted, bachelor uncle who worked for the city of Phoenix, received the array of mail order catalogs he did. Nick's mother was the one who went through her brother's place after he passed away, snapping up all the personal items, supposedly doing

Amy Kristoff

Nick a favor. Since Uncle Ted was found unconscious there by a neighbor, before being taken to the hospital where he later died, it almost seemed like there was some possible evidence. Nick had offered to help her, but she was adamant she do it herself. She'd happened to have been named in her brother Ted's will as some sort of personal representative, which Nick had taken to mean he had no say-so, despite having inherited the condo property. Besides, regarding his mother, if she was even lurking in the background, it was never long before she managed to surge to the front. Something about her . . . This sounded callous, but Nick always felt like she put herself first no matter what and that caused Nick's father to kill himself, unless he did so, accidentally.

Meanwhile, Nick's mother inherited a generous sum when her husband as well as her brother passed away. Finally she realized a seemingly long-lost dream and purchased a small hotel in Santa Fe, New Mexico. She moved there full-time earlier in the year, having finally sold her house here in the Phoenix area. However, despite having a time-consuming business to run, she still found time to return on occasion, for whatever reason.

Moving was out of the question for Nick. Despite his fear of spiders, he liked the climate here too much to go anywhere else. Besides, he had no intention of quitting his job and starting all over again. If anything, he'd have to start his own business so he could work for himself. A certain aspect of his job was really stressing him out, in the form of a co-worker, Greg Mortenski.

Increasingly, Mortenski was why Nick couldn't wait to leave work for the day, yet he formerly stayed late. His remedy was to bring some work home and it had nothing to do with trying to win points from their boss, Cal Mertz. Nick was addicted to work! So yes, he did deserve the promotion instead of Mortenski. But that was only because Nick had no other life! He'd never married nor had any kids . . . He hadn't even dated for a couple months, ever since having an "amicable break-up" with his girlfriend, Diane Waltzer. Looking back, she was like the one that got away. But since they'd agreed to part ways after close to a year of dating, maybe it was for the best. Still, he thought about her a lot.

Misanthropes ran in the family on Nick's mother's side, and he was starting to believe he had more in common with Uncle Ted than he had any idea. Suffice to mention, Nick never spent any time with the guy, even though his mother was close to her brother, growing up. Obviously Uncle Ted liked to have his space, something Nick appreciated. It was possible they even shared a fear of spiders, particularly tarantulas. It didn't help, Nick had yet to actually encounter one. He was fanatical about having an exterminator visit his residence at least once a month. If a company balked at coming "too often," he simply called another. The expense was no object, even though it wasn't like he was well-off. And his uncle's condo was vacant for quite awhile following his death. At one point, Nick even thought he was going to have to sell it and remain where he was, because of the added expenses of living in a much more upscale place. It also began to look doubtful he could sell his former property.

After ordering his tarantula computer mouse online, Nick specified overnight delivery, surprising himself with this sense of urgency. Then again, why not? He'd rather face his fears sooner than later. Besides, he was bored as hell. Anything to look forward to was fine with him.

Maybe some of this anticipation had to do with wanting a dog his entire childhood but never being allowed to have one. Time after time he'd pleaded his case, only to be told, "Not now," by his mother. At last count, she finally declared, "You can't. I'm allergic to them." Just like that! By that time Nick's father had been deceased a couple years. Nick had never asked him about acquiring a dog because his mother was always saying, "Don't bother your father."

It was very depressing, losing one parent to suicide, while

the other was severely lacking in maternal instincts. As much as Nick tried to accept his mother for who she was, he could never feel comfortable around her, even though she raised him. Sometimes he felt like he grew up in spite of her.

This place that was formerly Uncle Ted's did in fact allow dogs, as long as they weighed less than fifty pounds. Nick wouldn't want to have to pick up after a dog larger than that, anyway. Besides, no one in this gated community had much of a yard, other than what was enclosed in a courtyard.

Perhaps he could adopt a dog from the shelter. Since he'd been bringing more and more work home, essentially fleeing the office by five, Nick would have more opportunities to keep a new companion company.

It was impossible to pin Nick's hatred of Greg Mortenski on any one aspect. All Nick had to do was think about the guy and in turn became nauseous. If Mortenski had any idea the influence he had . . . Nick tried his damnedest not to lose it around him, but those days were numbered. Nick's hatred of Greg had nothing to do with their "competition" for a promotion because Nick was simply more qualified, which couldn't be emphasized enough. If their boss picked Mortenski instead of him, it was the company's loss.

What really floored Nick was the fact Mortenski was "a family guy" with a wife and two young kids yet acted so immature! Besides, he was only thirty or thirty-one to Nick's thirty-nine. There was no jealousy on Nick's part (he'd already carefully deliberated over that possibility). If he had ever envisioned "marriage and kids," that notion was long gone.

The bottom line was Nick needed to quit worrying about having Greg Mortenski seemingly constantly hazing him. Nick had to stand up for himself, no matter how juvenile the whole thing was.

As soon as Nick arrived at work the next morning, he

went to the break room to get a cup of coffee. His coffeemaker must have broken because it didn't have his coffee ready when he got up. He was running late, so he left the problem for when he returned home – after he unwrapped his new computer mouse, assuming it would be there later.

Nick usually arrived at work just before nine, while most everyone else came in around nine-thirty. He liked to get settled in his corner and be busy working by then. That way, when it was time to take a break, he was ready to do so, versus being tempted to work some more.

Just as Nick rounded the turn, holding a brimming Styrofoam cup of hot black coffee, about to reach the corner where his desk was located (versus the typical cubicle), Greg Mortenski "accidentally" collided with him. Not for a second did Nick believe as much. Meanwhile his white dress shirt and navy silk tie were soaked with his own coffee. Both were ruined, but the important part was the tie had been a Christmas gift from his ex-girlfriend, Diane. It wasn't inexpensive, and she didn't exactly have a high-salaried job, yet she obviously thought enough of their relationship to splurge on a holiday gift.

Mortenski feigned an apology by saying, "Sorry there, Farris. I didn't see you," all the while appearing as if he would break into uncontrollable laughter any second. Then he looked around as if trying to find something to help clean up the mess he'd made.

"Don't worry about it," Nick told him, just wanting to "Come on, Nick," Mortenski said, making a furtive effort to stop Nick from essentially fleeing.

Using every bit of his self-control, Nick managed to refrain from dumping the remainder of his coffee right on the one who deserved it most. Instead he headed for the restroom, hoping to clean up the best he could. It was going to be a very long day. In the meantime Mortenski had better keep away.

Finally on his way home, Nick realized there was a distinct possibility the box containing his tarantula-mouse wouldn't be on the front stoop because the delivery driver would refuse to leave it unless someone was present to sign for it. In other words, Nick would have to wade through another work day before receiving it. That was too long to wait! He'd first have to endure another eight-hour shift with Greg Mortenski and his itinerary of pranks and high-jinks.

All this ridiculousness proved it was imperative Nick "win" the promotion instead of Greg Mortenski. It was the only bolstering Nick could hope to receive for "combating" the guy. Obviously it was a competition, like it or not. If Nick was in fact promoted, thereby making Mortenski a subordinate, hopefully that would compel the idiot to quit.

The box was right by the front door, so Nick had needlessly worried about it. He'd spent his whole life either worrying about or bothered by non-issues. It was high time he change and resolved to finally do so. (Greg Mortenski being annoying non-stop, came to mind.)

Even though Nick wanted nothing more than to rip open the box, he vowed to change from his coffee-stained shirt into something clean and more comfortable. The ruined tie had been removed at work, although he didn't throw it away because of its sentimental value.

In his upstairs bedroom, about to change, the phone rang. Hardly anyone knew Nick's land line number, which was unlisted. Then his mother came to mind; he hadn't heard from her in awhile.

Sure enough it was her. As soon as Nick picked up, she dove right in, asking, "Nicki, how have you been?"

Nick could hardly reply, so incensed was he, she'd slipped and called him the hated "Nicki." She knew not to do that but somehow couldn't resist!

After finally mumbling he was doing fine, Nick's mother forged right ahead, saying, "I've been concerned about you lately, so I called to make sure you're all right. Also, I wanted to let you know I'm going to be in town in a couple days, and

I'd like to see you. I'm already booked for Christmas and won't be able to visit then, like I wanted."

Only at this point in her life did Nick's mother realize what a lousy job she did, raising him. But it was a matter of too little, too late, and it'd become instinctive to keep her at arm's length, despite her feeble attempts to appear interested in him and his welfare.

Nick told her, "I keep telling you to e-mail me. That way you don't have to call and call, hoping I answer . . . I set up your e-mail none other than last Christmas when I visited. Remember?"

"Yes, I do. You barely stayed, certainly not long enough to spend the night. And I'd reserved my best room for you. I had to turn potential guests away that holiday weekend, something I wasn't prepared for."

"You want to be reimbursed so you'll finally shut up?"

"I beg your pardon?"

"You heard me. You just can't believe I would talk to you like that," Nick said, literally trembling. He wasn't entirely surprised by his sudden lack of respect for his mother, if only because he'd wanted "to tell her off" for as long as he could remember. However, what undid him was the cause: he was so obsessed with opening the box containing his new computer mouse, he could hardly stand it – and her phone call was eating into his precious time!

As his mother stammered and sobbed, Nick callously told her, "I've got a lot to do right now, so just call me when you get in town and maybe we can go out to lunch or something. Bye."

Only after the call had ended did Nick realize he'd possibly gone overboard with his rudeness. Nonetheless, he felt no remorse – or not enough to waste time calling her back and apologizing. If anything, she owed him an apology, all for being his mother!

Finally changed into more comfortable clothes, Nick was ready to open the contents of the much-anticipated box, which was waiting for him on the kitchen counter.

Waiting for him? What the hell kind of remark was that? Maybe it was indeed time for a dog. If nothing else, this tarantula-mouse was really doing a number on him.

The tarantula-mouse was just as breath-taking in person as it appeared in the catalog (and online). Nick was so mesmerized by the hairy, dark brown, long-legged arachnid encased in acrylic, he sat in the kitchen for a good half-hour, staring at it. Even though he had plenty to do on the computer, he couldn't get himself to move.

Then his phone rang again, his cell phone this time. Thankfully he'd left it nearby, on the counter. Glancing at the number, Nick wasn't sure if he recognized it, yet it seemed like he should.

"Nick? It's Diane," his ex-girlfriend said when he mumbled "hello."

It was pleasantly surprising for Nick to hear from a woman he only broke up with because he'd wanted it to be "mutual." That way, at a time like this, he wouldn't want her too badly. Of course, that was before he'd discovered this computer mouse, which was the ultimate distraction from his relationship with an ex-girlfriend he'd thought was "The One."

In spite of desperately wanting to put his new mouse to use, Nick exchanged small-talk with Diane for a couple minutes before she unexpectedly invited herself over! One thing Nick had always liked was her lack of timidity, yet he wouldn't have described her as aggressive. After almost a year of dating, maybe he never knew her very well.

Nick put her off by first asking, "Aren't you seeing anyone? Or should I say 'sleeping with' anyone?" In turn, he had to hand it to her, she did an excellent job of sounding convincing when saying "no" and pretended not to be offended by the intrusive question. As much as he wanted to believe her, he couldn't, especially since he was looking for an excuse to end the call.

Diane proceeded to ask him, "How about tomorrow? I'd really like to see you, Nick."

After agreeing he might be available tomorrow after work (but she needed to call first), Nick positively hated himself. He knew exactly what she wanted and he felt the same way. They were only human, yet it was too humiliating to bear sometimes. He actually wished he were something else, ridiculous though that was.

Back to the tarantula-mouse. If it was truly dead, wouldn't its legs be curled up? Or was it killed and then its legs stretched back straight before rigor mortis set in? That was awfully cruel. It was time to get to work or he'd just sit here, staring and feeling awful about the fate of a tarantula, sacrificed for the sake of creating a unique computer mouse.

The next morning at work, Nick didn't bother to get a cup of coffee from the break room, although he'd failed to fix (or replace) his coffeemaker and was really hurting for some caffeine. Last evening, he'd spent so much time on his computer, basically goofing around once he'd finished his work, he didn't go to bed until almost midnight! He hadn't stayed up that late in ages. He had his new mouse to thank. At the same time, it was unbelievable his fear of spiders was completely overcome in the meantime. Therefore, if he did encounter an actual tarantula in his house, he'd probably have a heart attack, but for the time being he felt more at ease than he'd been in years. He was even willing to cancel his next exterminator appointment, as another company had recently made a service call.

So what happened was Nick nearly overslept and didn't end up arriving at the office until later than his usual "early time." He didn't want a replay of the day before, when Greg Mortenski "accidentally" bumped into him. It couldn't have been mentioned enough, the guy had a mental problem if he thought it was funny to torment Nick. The real dig was how the two of them were in contention for the same promotion-position.

It seemed awfully quiet around the office, Nick realized after he'd been working for a couple hours. Then it occurred to him, Mortenski had yet to show up. He couldn't have because he never failed to at least stop by Nick's corner for a second or two, just for the sake of showing his mug. Who did suddenly show up but Nick's (and Mortenski's) boss, Cal Mertz.

After exchanging pleasantries, Mr. Mertz told Nick, "I'd like to have a word with you in my office, Nick. By the way, Greg won't be in today or even the rest of the week. His wife went into labor late last night and a couple hours ago gave birth to a seven-pound baby girl they named Hannah."

Nick just nodded. He was pretty sure Mortenski's wife's name was Karen, but Nick sure as hell had no idea she was pregnant with yet another kid. Obviously Mortenski had his hands full at home, so why the hell would he pick on anyone? Didn't he have enough to do?

Once in his boss' office, Nick couldn't help glancing around, even though it wasn't the first time he'd been in here. It never ceased to amaze him, how luxurious a mere office could be. Nick was just glad he wasn't in here to be given the boot. Or so he hoped.

Barely was Nick seated in a plush, black leather chair facing his boss' gargantuan oak desk when he was told, "Nick, I appreciate your dedication to this company, including willingly working extra hours at home, but for the imminent future, I'm going to have to hold off making a decision regarding who should be promoted to handle an additional tier of this company. The economy appears to be gradually improving, but I feel it'd be for everyone's benefit if I extend a wait-and-see approach."

Hearing the news, Nick wasn't sure what to think. What

he did know was he wanted to leave for the rest of the day. Then again, since Mortenski was gone for the remainder of the week, it should have been cause for celebration. It was only Tuesday, so Nick wouldn't have to see the guy again for close to a week. Nonetheless, something didn't feel right. Maybe he was secretly dreading Diane's "probable arrival" at his place later, following her "required" phone call. (She knew him well enough to heed his wishes, despite how stipulating they were.)

Somehow Nick made it through the work day. He never thought it could have been so difficult, even knowing Mortenski wasn't around to pop up seemingly out of nowhere. Once he was home again, Nick left his mail on the kitchen counter before heading upstairs to change into more comfortable clothes. Unlike yesterday, at least what he'd worn to work wasn't ruined by a huge, dried coffee stain. However, Nick didn't intend to exact any revenge. Then he'd definitely kill his chances of "winning" the promotion (which he couldn't help keeping in mind and continued to consider himself the more favorable candidate).

Before heading upstairs, Nick couldn't resist going to his office/den and looking at his beloved new computer mouse. To think, he'd used it for hours the day before, and there'd been a tarantula beneath his right hand the entire time! Getting over this phobia was not only fun but inspiring.

The acrylic mouse was on the pine desk, but there was no tarantula encased in it – or no longer in it was more like it. Absolutely impossible. Even if the arachnid was indeed still alive when it was placed in the acrylic mold, there was no possible way it could have survived for long, let alone somehow disappeared.

After staring at the mouse for a few minutes, Nick began looking around the room, with its many places for a spider to hide, including the bookshelves lining the wall to the right of his desk, which faced a sliding glass door, leading to a canopied courtyard. Then again, wouldn't a spider, particularly a tarantula, prefer to live outside?

A couple more minutes of glancing around the room, and Nick took one more look at the "empty" computer mouse before hurrying upstairs to change. He didn't even want to come back downstairs. What he wanted to do was go to bed, wake up, and find he'd dreamed all this.

There was only so long she, Diane Waltzer, intended to remain single. By 39, she'd fully expected to be married and staying home, versus working at whatever dead-end career it might be. She gave up even thinking about having kids (but she wasn't very maternal anyway). Initially she'd made a couple blunders, pursuing men who were too far above her (bosses). To top it off, even if she could have managed a brief affair with any of them, every single one was "happily married" (not planning on divorcing his wife and marrying Diane), so she forced herself to be realistic and amazingly enough ended up with a real find, in the form of Nick Farris. It was her fault they'd broken up; she'd gotten tired of his eccentricities. However, as soon as she found herself alone again (and no new dating prospects in sight), she had an opportunity to obsess over every aspect of their relationship. A couple months after their break-up, she'd been compelled to call him. In turn, she'd been encouraged by the fact he actually answered the phone and was willing to see her but put her off for one day.

That was why Diane was calling Nick again, expecting to be given the go-ahead to pay him a visit. If it wasn't already made clear, she always managed to get what she wanted, one way or another. If he didn't answer, she intended to just show up at his place. She'd make sure to wear some sexy undergarments and would expect Nick wanted to see her but was being aloof. She didn't take it personally, knowing him pretty well.

Nick answered the phone when his expected call came from Diane. He couldn't afford to blow her off because she'd simply show up, something he did not want. Besides, he really needed someone to talk to right now because he felt as if he'd gone insane! Realistically, it wasn't a complete surprise, given how he'd been a loner his whole life – not just in adulthood. As much as Nick wanted to settle down, perhaps he simply couldn't.

"What are you doing right now?" Diane coyly asked Nick after they'd exchanged hellos.

Still too freaked-out about his "missing tarantula" to appreciate Diane's tone of voice, Nick glumly replied, "I'd been planning on getting some work done that I'd brought home from the office, but something really strange just happened, so now I don't feel like doing much of anything."

"Are you *sure*?"

"At this point, Diane, until I get some answers about what I just saw or only imagined . . . Forget it. I can't explain this whole mess over the phone."

"So let me come over."

"All right. Why not," Nick told his ex-girlfriend. Diane always thought she deserved exactly what she wanted. Same with his mother. And their determination to have total control luckily went hand-in-hand with the unexpected need for a "missing tarantula" to have a sacrifice or two. He'd done some research on North American tarantulas, and they in fact pursued their prey, versus wasting time and effort spinning a web. Genius! A tarantula was smarter than a person, not really a surprise.

For starters Nick would just wait for Diane to show up and follow his tarantula-friend's cue.

CPSIA information can be obtained
at www.ICGtesting.com
Printed in the USA
FFOW02n1216250516
24425FF